Caught Dead
in Philadelphia

Caught Dead in Philadelphia

GILLIAN ROBERTS

CHARLES SCRIBNER'S SONS · NEW YORK

Copyright © 1987 by Judith Greber

Charles Scribner's Sons
Macmillan Publishing Company
866 Third Avenue, New York, N.Y. 10002
Collier Macmillan Canada, Inc.

This is a work of fiction. Names, characters, places, and incidents either are the product of the author's imagination or are used fictitiously. Any resemblance to actual events or persons, living or dead, is entirely coincidental.

Printed in the United States of America

This, too,
is Robert's

Caught Dead in Philadelphia

One

AT 7:58 A.M. ON A WET MONDAY MORNING, twenty-seven hours after giving up cigarettes and a green-eyed disc jockey, I was not in a mood to socialize. Facing myself in the bathroom mirror had exhausted my conviviality. Choosing a sweater and skirt had used up my intellectual reserve.

Nonetheless, the doorbell rang. I wasn't expecting any deliveries. The *Philadelphia Inquirer* had already arrived, hurled at the house with such vengence its front page was gashed. So much for scheduled guests.

The only unexpected deliveries I receive are Nice Young Men sent C.O.D. by relatives who cannot bear the stigma of a thirty-year-old spinster schoolmarm in the family. I have tried to end their shipments by sending them clippings, statistics on delayed marriage and child-bearing. I've tried to convince them that it's un-American, not to mention unfashionable, to rush into anything except high-tech careers.

They respond by sending more Nice Young Men. But the N.Y.M. don't arrive in the mornings, anyway.

I shuffled to the front door and stared through the peephole. The act was a formality. The peephole tilted upward, like a telescope. With it I could sight the Big Dipper at appropriate times of the year, but that was all.

"Mandy? Open up! Please! It's me, Liza."

"Liza who?"

"Liza Nichols."

Surprised and puzzled, I opened the door onto Liza and the monsoon season. I was willing to lose a little of a rushed morning to find out why a near stranger would visit at this hour. Liza bolted past me, then slowed down, dribbling a damp trail around the room that serves as my kitchen, dining, and living room. She tossed her raincoat over my suede chair, shaking her black hair like a puppy. She was of the perfect-featured, small sort men treat like children or dolls, but at the moment she looked pasty instead of porcelain skinned.

"Thank God you're here!" she exclaimed. "Don't know what I'd have done otherwise."

I discreetly removed the raincoat and brushed off the chair. I am not a fanatic housekeeper, but suede is impractical at best, and sopping raincoats are definitely off-limits. And now that I'd given up the disc jockey— and maybe more important, cigarettes—the chair was my only impractical and unwise love object.

I waited for a clue as to why Liza was in my living room at this ungodly hour. She shouldn't have appeared in my life until shortly after two o'clock, and then it should have been in my classroom. Liza was a co-worker, not a friend. She was a part-time teacher of creative dramatics. She was a very good actress, on-stage and off, although she was about to take early retirement from playing other people's scripts when she married in three weeks. Along with all the rest of the

English faculty, I had been at her engagement party a few weeks earlier, a joyless affair that was easy to confuse with a press conference. But perhaps I am unfair. Or jealous. Liza was marrying one of the most proper and wealthy of Philadelphians, a candidate—and likely winner—for state senator, and after that, judging by his demeanor, King of America.

"I'm exhausted," she said in her stagy manner. "Got off the bus and walked for hours. I didn't know where to go. If I hadn't remembered you lived on Litton, if your house hadn't been right here..." She collapsed extravagantly onto my sofa and leaned back against the cushions.

"What bus? From where? Why?"

She waved away my logical questions in an irritating queen-bee manner.

I put her coat on the radiator, discounted most of what she'd said—she was, as I said, fond of dramatic overstatement—and dared one more inhospitable question. "Liza, what brings you here?" I picked up my coffee cup and sipped the lukewarm brew.

"I need time," she said between a sneeze and a yawn. "Have to think. Can't go home. My mother's impossible. Always was, but she's worse since the engagement. Worried that I'll blow it. Wants me to regain my virginity before the wedding. Anyway, this is a good place. I always tell her I'm here when I'm going to be out all night."

I put down my coffee cup. "You tell her what?"

"You don't mind, do you?" she asked, with no real interest in how I might feel about it. "See, my mother—"

But, as if it had heard the maternal password, the telephone rang. "Coffee, Liza?" I finally asked, because she was eyeing my cup, looking like a hungry, wet poodle. Besides, the question delayed answering the call, and I knew, in the damp center of my bones, who it had to be.

My mother always seems surprised that I answer my own phone, although I live alone. "Amanda?" she asks, terrified that a man might answer and she'd have to decide whether she was outraged or delighted. She was unsure enough to have gone through a person-to-person phase, but while that protected her innocence, it was too expensive. She switched to a discount service with horrible reception.

My mother calls because she thinks that if she pounds the word "marriage" on my head, repeats her basic message—"Get Married!"—enough times, and emphasizes the time requirement—"Get Married Soon!"—I'll buckle under. And she has chosen early Monday mornings, she says, because I'm too hard to reach other times. I say it's because she figures that with my resistance low anyway at the start of another week of spoiled and dull-witted adolescents ("other people's children," as she subtly calls them), I'll be receptive to her message. And then she'll have one of her sisters ship over another Nice Young Man.

"I'd love some," Liza said, and I was hard pressed to remember what she meant until she added, "coffee."

I nodded. My mother chirruped greetings from Florida. She had been up all night with insomnia.

"All I really need is to talk to somebody," Liza said from the couch. My mother had the same need, and she took precedence. She began cataloging the condition of her various body parts. I held the phone on my shoulder, set out another coffee cup, and waited for the water to boil. Mama progressed from sciatica to hemorrhoids. I opened a can of cat food and put its contents in a bowl on the floor.

"Milk?" I whispered in Liza's direction. Unfortunately, my mother's ears are not one of her afflicted parts, and she cut short her analysis of hot flashes to question me about the milk drinker.

"A friend from school, Mother. Female." I don't know whether my answer disappointed or relieved her. "Liza," I added, "the one I told you about. Who's marrying Hayden Cole, remember?" Mother made impressed coos. I had won a few points by being in the same room with a person who believed in marriage.

"You know how sometimes you think you're so smart?" Liza said, more or less to herself. She nodded her head, then shook it. "Then you find out you're a stupid..." Perhaps she had rushed to me after flunking an all-night IQ test. She nervously tapped her nails against her bottom teeth, fiddled with a locket at her neck, and twisted her engagement ring. "And the two of them..."

I held up a finger, trying to signal Liza to wait for true confessions until I was finished with Mama. Liza sighed and seemed to shrink. She lit a cigarette.

I tried to inhale whatever smoke drifted my way. I certainly missed cigarettes more than the disc jockey. But then, I'd quit smoking cold turkey, and quit him only after whatever we'd had was long since dead.

"Sugar?" I whispered. Liza held up two fingers. Her metabolism worked overtime. I dumped a pack of carcinogenic sweetener in my own cup.

Since my coffee partner was not a prospective husband, my mother reminded me that I wasn't getting any younger. I listened, meanwhile filling the cups with brown powder and boiling water.

My mother informed me that it was a sunny eighty-four degrees down there.

Liza sneezed.

I resent my parents' metamorphosis into leathery sybarites. When they sold their house up here, they sold out, donating their boots, loyalty, and Puritan ethics to Goodwill. Florida had frizzed their brains, made them forget that weather is to be endured, not enjoyed.

Too sweetly, my mother asked me for a local report. She knew about April in Philadelphia. Had anyone ever written a song about it?

A sheet of windblown rain slid down the front window, breaking into fine patterns on the many panes. "It's a little humid here, Mom," I said. "And Mom? I have to go now. Time to leave for work."

My mother remained unperturbed. She asked if I'd ever considered a dating service. She had heard about an actual matchmaker, very modernized, complete with computers. Since I seemed unable to end the conversation, I tried to be a good hostess. I "ummed" while Mama told me not to knock something before I tried it. I squeezed the receiver between my shoulder and ear and walked over to the sofa with Liza's coffee.

The coffee made it, some of it even inside the cup. But the telephone cord lassoed the milk carton, the sugar bowl, and my coffee on the kitchen counter. I heard the crash and returned to find everything in a new and dismaying pattern on the kitchen floor, slopping over the cat food.

I would like to think I'll eventually outgrow the gawky stage.

My mother let me get on with my life. After all, if I wasn't going to move South or find a husband, I'd better hang on to my job.

"Don't clean it up," Liza said as I replaced the receiver. "I'll do it."

"That's okay. No problem." I picked up the dripping milk carton.

"Please, Amanda? Please?" The urgency in her voice startled me. "Talk to me instead." She lit a second cigarette. "I'm so mixed up, and you're so together, so self-sufficient. You know what you want, what to do. . . ."

Liza was not an ace at judging character, but I didn't contradict her. I stepped over the slop and went into the living room.

"I really look up to you," she said.

"That's because I'm taller."

"My mother's no help."

I didn't like being categorized with the previous generation. I'm older than Liza, but only chronologically. If half her anecdotes were true, she'd lived her quarter-century double-time.

I hid my annoyance by putting on lipstick, a darker shade than normal. I'm aware that I've been given a fair share by nature, and I basically like myself. I like being tall. I like my hair, although I sometimes wish it would decide whether it's red or brown. I've also got great knees, but that doesn't count for much. As for the rest of me, even on my worst days I know that I'm not likely to turn any viewers into stone.

But when I'm around Liza's miniaturized voluptuousness, her shiny black hair and smooth white skin, I feel oversized and drab. Even today, when she was at her worst.

So I boosted my color quotient with extra makeup. When I can afford analysis, I'll work out the deeper meaning of these ego problems. In the meantime, blusher is cheap.

Liza exhaled great gusts of smoke. Every time she filled the air with that comforting old stench, I had problems remembering what I was trying to prove by quitting. "I'd do what I want," she said abruptly, "if I knew what it was. If everybody would lay off, stop offering advice. Everybody has answers, but I don't know if they're my answers. How do you know?"

"Me? I don't. But I know what you mean. I just broke up with somebody who kept telling me what I wanted and who I was, and—"

"Jesus, what a number she did! What did I ever do to her? And then he—I mean what if it's a lie? How do I know if she—?"

It sounded like one of my mother's bad connections. Either I was hearing every third word or Liza was less than coherent. In any case, my nerve endings and professional pride couldn't withstand her indefinite pronouns.

"Liza, who? Who is he? And for that matter, who is she? Your mother?"

"My mother?" She looked startled and bemused. "What does my mother have to do with...? Oh, Lord, do I sound nuts? I'm just tired. More than tired, I'm..." She looked close to tears. Then she shrugged. "Tired. That's all. Forget it. You'll be late for work."

"I have a few minutes."

"Thanks, anyway." Her bright smile looked pasted on. "It isn't really anything I can discuss. I guess I got flustered in the rain and dark, but I'll handle it. If you'll let me stay, I'll nap, and my head will straighten out. That's all I need." She continued beaming beatifically, but her nervous fingers worked on her damp hair, her neck, her green T-shirt.

I did have to get to work. Still, I put on my raincoat

reluctantly. It was not yet 9:00 A.M., and I had already failed at something.

She pulled the afghan around her and stretched out on the sofa. "You'll be at the two o'clock class, won't you?" I asked, needing reassurance.

"Sure. I won't stand you up this time." Then she grinned. "But I'll stand up. Properly. Complete with bra."

"What does that have to do with anything?"

"Last time I was in, the office witch gave me a memo about undergarments. Teachers, even part-time, are not allowed to have nipples." She grinned. "Get going," she insisted. "I have to sleep. Forget my mood. I have."

I locked up with the uneasy feeling that her smile and her great drowsiness were masks she'd remove the moment I left her alone.

By one o'clock, my Monday lunch hour, my stomach walls were huddled together, praying for something to digest. I tried to bribe them with the polyethylene soufflé of the day, but after a few bites, I decided to fast.

"I'm going upstairs to mark papers," I said.

"The food's not that bad," Gus Winston answered. "Kind of tickles when it bounces around inside. Anyway, keep me company."

He smiled. I love his face, a mobile, slightly eroded sand sculpture. I looked at my dog-eared stack of ungraded compositions, knowing that as soon as they were marked, double their numbers would spring up in their place. "Maybe I'll get some of it done next period while Liza teaches."

"In that case, work now. Never rely on Liza. For

anything." Gus was the resident Liza expert. They worked together at a semiprofessional repertory theater. They had done other things together, very briefly, but that history had left him with more scars than Vietnam had.

"She promised."

"She always does, doesn't she? That's easy for her. It's harder remembering the promise a whole week later."

"But this was this morning. In my own living room."

Gus put down his fork. "I didn't think you had coffee klatches at dawn. Or was it the morning after a pajama party?"

"I don't know what it was. The rain washed her in this morning."

Gus chewed the last of his soufflé meditatively. Vietnam had ruined his left leg, scarred his face, and narrowed his acting ambitions, but it obviously hadn't touched his digestive tract. "Is she still at your house?" he asked.

"Probably. She wanted to nap. Why?"

"We—I have to talk to her. Tried to last night, after the show, but she was having one of her tantrums."

"She was odd this morning, too. What's up?"

"You tell me. I don't understand a goddamn thing about Liza Nichols. Hasn't she told you that? She's told everybody else." He stabbed his red square of Jell-O and watched it shudder before pushing it away, his fork sinking in its heart. "I hear she's being coached on how to fit into Hayden Cole's once-and-future life. How to dress, talk, change her style. Senators can be prima donnas, but their wives are supposed to serve tea and smile on the sidelines."

"Patience, Gus. She isn't a wife yet. And he isn't a senator, either."

"Details. She'll be his missus in three weeks, and he'll either win the state or buy it, just as he already bought Liza."

There was nothing for me to say. Gus hadn't gotten what he expected from life or Liza Nichols, and I couldn't do a thing about either situation.

He muttered in semitheatrical fashion. Too softly to be understood and too loudly to be ignored.

"Speak up or shut up, Gus. All I hear is smidgies, and it's making me crazy—sissies and stupids? Sounds like preschool."

"Sissie Bellinger. Remember her? Skinny blonde who was at the engagement party. It's all her fault. It was her idea to have a benefit show for Hayden Cole, to drag in half the Main Line at one hundred dollars a seat. And how could anybody object? Sissie's one of the biggest backers—patrons—of the Playhouse. Frustrated actress herself. She hangs out there half the time, driving everybody up the wall while she supervises her write-off. Damn her."

He stood up and limped toward the collection bin. I followed with my full tray, trying not to think of the wide-eyed kids in the starvation ads who would die for want of what I scraped off my plate.

"Benefit! Certainly didn't benefit Liza. She meets Mr. Candidate and kisses off everything she's worked and hoped for. Good-bye, New York, acting. Hello, Hayden, the hope of the bland people."

"Don't you think you're making a bit much of this? Maybe it's what she wanted all along."

"Hayden?" He slammed down his tray. "Hayden Cole? Maybe his money. Maybe his power. Maybe his status. Maybe just the ego-pumping thrill of being invited to share it. But Hayden himself? You've seen him—he could be her father, practically. Looks like a desiccated— Maybe I wasn't what she wanted, okay. Maybe I don't understand her. But I understand enough to know she never wanted any Hayden Cole!"

We climbed the stairs together. Neither the food nor the conversation had turned lunch into a leisurely affair, and there were forty minutes left before my last class. I could get some papers marked.

"I think I'll have a smoke," Gus said. "Coming along?"

"I don't smoke."

"Again?" He looked at his watch. "I'll try to catch Liza at the end of next period. If she shows."

"She'd better." It was the only aspect of Liza that concerned me at the moment.

Gus once designed a coat of arms for our school. On a shield of rulers and pencils rested a dunce cap. Below it, in elegant calligraphy read the legend: Philadelphia Prep: For the Rich and the Retarded. It was not adopted as the official school emblem, despite its hard kernel of truth. Our building, an imposing center-city mansion, is far more impressive than our students' minds. However, I am still not sure what I want to be when—or if—I grow up, and since my liberal arts degree does not include the courses in audiovisual aids and such that give you public school teaching credentials, I try not to make too much fun of Philly Prep because its slack admission policy provides me with students to teach and the means to pay my rent.

I sat at my desk marking compositions. I fought the urge to retreat from the plodding sentences, but eventually I lost, and I put my head down, wondering why I didn't inspire my classes the way Liza did. I liked to think it was because I was always there and Liza was an unreliable and sporadic treat. In any case, she made plays come alive and her delight was contagious.

She was currently generating interest in *Macbeth* with a class of seniors. They had only two months of school left, and they had never known a scholarly urge in the first place. Their grades were long since submitted to colleges, their fates by and large determined, and the two remaining months of school were no more than glorified day care in their eyes. Even so, they listened to Liza and to William Shakespeare. Until you've faced a crowd of graduating seniors, you have not experienced apathy and cannot appreciate the heroic and historic feat Liza had accomplished.

She was very involved with her work. "I'd like to rewrite this play," she'd told me once of *Macbeth*. "With a more sympathetic Lady M. She wasn't a bad old girl. No different from the rest of us, really. She wanted to get somewhere in life. She was just clumsy and overly moral, carrying on like that. She should have hung around until the crown settled onto her head. Once it was old, she wouldn't have gotten bad press."

"Come on," I'd protested. "There were a few murders on her record."

"You're naive, Amanda. Once you've arrived, it doesn't matter how you got there. People don't peep behind the stacks of money. Hayden's handsome trust was built on shaky land grants, Yankee slave ships, a lot of dead Indians, and God knows what else. But it happened long ago. So who cares now? Who cared twenty years ago when his daddy was governor? Time washes off the blood, Mandy."

She paced around, thinking. "For example, my engagement ring. You'd be upset if you thought I'd stolen it. But if it's an antique—if it was stolen a few generations ago, would anybody care? See this locket? Hayden's mother gave it to me, and you should have seen the ceremony attached to the presentation."

She hunched over, transforming her curvaceous body into a sexless, heavy mass. "Liza, dear," she said in a low, nasal voice, "this was Grandmother Lucy Bolt Hayden's, and then her son, my father, Benjamin Sedgewick Hayden, gave it to my mother, and my mother gave it to me. Now you are to have it, and someday..."

Liza straightened up and became herself again. "Now where did Gramma Lucy get it, do you suppose? Her daddy probably dumped a shipload of slaves down South and blew part of the profits on a trinket for his kid. Does anybody care if this locket cost a life? Time has cleaned it off."

She'd picked up the twelfth-grade anthology with *Macbeth* in it. "The point is, Lady Macbeth should have stuck it out. Silly fool, washing and washing those bloody hands, when all it took was time. She was much too moral."

The two o'clock bell jarred me out of my reveries. Students barreled through the door, looking for Liza.

Their disappointment was nothing compared to mine. I waited. I took roll. I simmered. Then I broke into a boil. Maybe now that Liza was moving into money and power, she could break the rules the rest of us followed.

But that didn't mean I couldn't protest. "Please read the play silently for a few minutes. I'm going to see if I can find Miss Nichols."

I charged down the hallway, hoping to bump into Liza. But I saw only Gus, closing his classroom door.

"The actress is AWOL," I snapped, as if his pessimis-

tic predictions had made it come true. I stormed past
him toward the school office. I wasn't sure what I
could accomplish, but I was angry and needed to let it
out on someone, somewhere.

But not on Helga Putnam, the office witch. As I
neared her, she pulled her gray cardigan tightly
around her shoulders as if suddenly chilled. She didn't
like her domain invaded by teachers. Or students. Or
parents.

"Miss Pepper!" Helga never wasted time on pleas-
antries. "I was about to send a messenger to your
room. When Miss Nichols completes her hour, send
her here. She hasn't signed in at the office, and we
cannot tolerate such unprofessional behavior!" Her
nose glowed at the tip in a red blotch of congealed
rage.

As furious as I was with Liza, I was not about to ally
myself with the harpy behind the desk. "I'll tell her," I
said. It wasn't really a lie. I would tell her—whenever
I could. I walked over to the telephone at the far end
of the room. A grid of mailboxes covered much of the
nearby wall. I'd emptied mine that morning, but it had
been fed more squares of paper, more of Helga's reminders about "professional behavior."

The mailbox labeled "L. Nichols" was overflowing
with old notices, new notices, and a small brown package. Since I'd already implied that Liza was in the
building, I surreptitiously emptied the contents of her
mailbox into my pocketbook.

My descent into a life of duplicity continued when I
picked up the office phone. I could feel Putnam's eyes
bore into my back, I could sense another memo about
personal-call vouchers. I pushed down the button and
spoke into the dead receiver. "Operator? What is the
area code for Fargo, North Dakota?" There was a gasp

behind me, then the scratch of pen on paper. "Of course I'll get the charges, Helga," I said without turning around.

"Thank you," I told the dead receiver, and then I dialed several numbers before I released the buttons, waited for a dial tone, and called my house. The phone rang fourteen times before I slammed it down. She wasn't there, then. She wasn't anywhere.

Helga snorted as I left the office.

My class was midway through a small war or bacchanal. "Back in your seats," I said. "We'll read the play together."

The room was overheated, and the rain on the windows lulled us all. The kids droned through their lines. It wasn't the same without the resident actress.

Lance Zittsner, who had trouble reading an Exit sign, stammered and spluttered through his part. "Bo—bloody instructions, which being taught, return to—" He looked up at me, sweating. "To plaque? Like on teeth?"

"To plague. 'We do but teach bloody instructions which, being taught, return to plague the inventor.' That means—"

But the 3:00 P.M. bell rang, and the students, passionately uninterested in my words or Shakespeare's, stampeded toward freedom. So much for anybody's bloody instructions.

I stood awhile at the rain-streaked windows. The bright slickers and umbrellas of escaping teenagers punctuated the square of park across the street. I adjusted the hems of my window shades. Philly Prep put great emphasis on keeping its rooms, if not its students, in pristine order.

When the building hushed with the unnatural quiet

of an empty school, I left, carrying a wad of still un-marked papers.

I walked behind the school and splashed through the puddles on the makeshift parking lot. At least, having been late this morning, I was the blockee, not the blocked. It didn't make me happy enough. I thought about Gene Kelly tap-dancing through a downpour. The thought mellowed me out all the way to Good Sa-maritanism. Gus's car, nosed against the wall in front of mine, had an open rear window. Rain funneled in onto his torn upholstery. I tried squeezing my hand through the opening to unlock the door. Then I tried all the other doors. Failure. I ended up with my roll book in a puddle, my head sopping, and the realization that, unlike me, Gene Kelly was given big bucks to make merry in the rain. So I drove home.

Or near home. I live on a cute street, as streets go. It has history, cobblestones, and hitching posts. It doesn't have parking. My lot is two blocks from home. This allows me to enjoy fully Philadelphia's range of weather conditions. In summer I can perspire pro-fusely. In winter I can cultivate chilblains. And on this particular spring Monday, I was able to determine how much moisture can seep through suede boots during an exhilarating jog.

Nothing happened when I turned the key. At first I thought my locks had been changed or I was losing my mind. Then I had a mental breakthrough, and I turned the key back in the other, wrong direction.

The door opened.

Liza had left the house unlocked. The magnitude of her irresponsibility overwhelmed me. I kicked the door all the way open, slammed it shut behind me, and sloshed toward the small closet at the back of the first floor. As I pulled off my raincoat, I caught a glimpse of the kitchen floor. The coffee, with sugar, cream, and cat food, was still there.

I felt enraged, and then defeated, because there was nothing to be done about people like that who left the work of the world up to people like me. I was cold and damp, and I had boring compositions to mark, and I vowed that when I saw Liza again, I'd—

But in midvow I turned back toward the living room and swallowed whatever threat was building. Because I saw Liza. Or part of her. A foot in a small gray shoe sticking out from the side of the sofa near the fireplace.

Odd, unconnected thoughts popped through my brain. Nobody naps in shoes. Strange position. No answer on telephone when I called. Unlocked door.

I moved in slow motion across the room.

Nobody naps on the hearth with a sofa nearby.

"Please, no." I heard myself say it, hoped Liza could hear it. "Please—"

Nobody naps on a hearth.

She lay crumpled and small, like a wrecked toy, her mouth half-open, her arms outstretched as if grasping for something to hold on to. Her green shirt was twisted, one jeans leg pulled up, showing a pale section of leg. Her dark eyes stared at me.

But they weren't her eyes. They were mannequin eyes, with no spark, no shine of life.

"No," I said, near tears. "Please, no!" I bent over her, hoping, insisting it was possible she was alive, almost convincing myself despite the discolored, scraped skin on her temple.

"No!" I screamed, putting my ear to her chest. "Please?" I listened, pressed, begged, found no pulse.

I shook her, shouting, as if I could insist her back to life. Then I stopped, remembering first aid rules. But

I shook her once again, anyway, and felt bile rise in my throat as her head wobbled lifelessly.

"Liza! Please!"

I stumbled to the telephone, bracing myself against the kitchen counter, fighting off a black circle swallowing me.

I pushed the first number of the police.

She was barefoot when I left. She put shoes on because somebody came here. She didn't fall. She put on shoes to greet somebody.

Somebody had been here. Pushed her. Didn't get help. Watched her die.

I put the receiver on the counter softly and stood in the narrow kitchen, listening.

My heartbeat echoed up the stairway, off the bedroom walls, reaching whom? Who still hid upstairs?

I could see Liza's small foot at the end of the living room, could hear nothing but the ragged edge of my own breath.

Off the hook, the receiver buzzed angrily. I stared at it, frozen, my mouth half-open, listening to the pulsing silence coming down the stairway.

"Help." My voice was a painful whisper. "Help."

I left the phone hanging and ran out into the rain. I stood on the front step a second, inhaling the wet air until my lungs again functioned. Then I ran.

TWO

I SAT ON THE SOFA QUIETLY, WATCHING THE two men inspect the fireplace.

The shorter of the two, a slender, burnt-almond man, stroked his thin mustache. "I don't need any lab boys to tell me that's blood on the stone." He crouched slightly. "Head height. She was a little thing. Maybe five feet two. She would have hit right about here." He straightened up. "You about done, man?" he asked his companion.

The other one seemed mesmerized. "Hmm?" he said, rousing himself. "Oh. No. Be a while longer. Want to clear a few things with Miss Peppah, heah."

His voice was gentle, softly Southern. It was nevertheless one voice too many for me, and it scraped across my nerves like sandpaper. I'd already told them everything I knew or knew how to say.

"I told the other officers, the ones here before you," I began.

"Yes," he drawled. "Yay-ess. I know." But he didn't budge.

"Then I'll start questioning the neighbors," the dark-skinned one said, pulling on an alpaca-lined raincoat.

"Not going to be worth anything. It'll just give them something to talk about during dinner. While I miss mine. Your street always this quiet, Miss Pepper? Looks like a damned museum. Ye Olde Colonial Philadelphia. No traffic, no people, no nothing." He didn't once look at me while he spoke. "Cobblestones!" He snorted as he walked to the door.

"Hey, Ray? After you finish the street, you'll get those addresses, right? I'll be out in twenty minutes or so." As he spoke, he walked over and settled himself in my suede chair, taking great pains to arrange his long legs.

Ray opened the front door. "How come you white boys get to sit in warm houses, man, and I get to walk up and down in the rain?" And he left, slamming the door behind him.

So. Almost everyone was finally gone. Liza was gone. The photographer was gone, the bluecoats, the man who measured everything, the man who sprinkled everything, and the two who had already questioned me—all the bodies, living and dead, who'd swarmed over and clogged up my house for hours were gone. All except this one, who was making himself very comfortable across from me.

"Don't you mind Raymond," he said, running his fingers through his curly, somewhat unkempt hair. "He's a man of reg-lar habits, and he dislikes working through his dinnertime. So do I, and, I presume, you don't like being bothered just now. But I do have some questions, so if you'd kindly explain one more time, I'd 'preciate it."

The slurred voice, the handsome features, the friendly expression, the relaxed and sociable pose didn't disguise the fact that he wasn't making a request, but a demand. Still, I didn't know what was left to say.

"Miss Peppah?" he prompted.

"I don't know what you want. I've said everything already. Several times. I came home and found—"

"Exactly when was that?"

"Around three forty-five."

"Where'd you go after school?"

"Nowhere."

"Miss Pepper." He seemed to remember his accent only sporadically. "Philadelphia Prep is ten blocks from here. The distance could be strolled in fifteen minutes. Why'd it take you forty-five minutes to drive it?"

"What kind of question is that? I stayed in my room awhile after school. Then it was raining. There were barriers up for potholes on Fifteenth Street. My parking lot is two blocks away. Why do I have to tell you this? What does it have to do with anything?"

He shrugged and fixed his pale blue eyes on me as if I were a dull specimen. "Is there anyone who can verify your stayin' after school?"

"What are you trying to say?"

"Didn't I say it clearly?"

I tried to stay calm. I had been trying for hours, with varying degrees of success. "I didn't see anybody," I snapped. "Why are you treating me this way? It was horrible enough finding her. Why are you treating me as if I—"

He loosened the edges of his mouth. I realized he wasn't much older than I was, despite the sprinkle of gray in his brown hair. And he wasn't really fierce looking. It was just that he was very tall, and having the entire force of the law behind him gave him an awesome stature.

"Sorry," he said in his soft, slow way. "I know it's rough on you. But at the risk of stating the obvious, I'm doing my job. I'm a detective. I detect. They give

us a list of questions to ask. If we don't ask them, they
take away our badges. So ease up—stop interpreting
my motives and humor me." He sighed and continued. "You say you got home at quarter to four, but we
didn't get the call until four-twenty. Why?"

"Mr.—Officer—Detective—sir—"

"Mackenzie. C. K. Mackenzie."

I am suspicious of people who hide inside little bun-
dles of letters, but I didn't think I should mention it at
this time. Anyway, this wasn't a person. This was an
inquisitor.

"Why didn't you call the police for forty minutes?"

"I told you. Or somebody."

He nodded, a Buddha with gray-brown curls, eyes
half-closed. "And?" he prompted.

"When I knew she was—"

"Yes?"

"I panicked. I started to call the police, but then I
was afraid that whoever—so I ran. To find help."

Retelling it, feeling the panic rise again, made me
stand up and walk around. But my place isn't large
enough for serious pacing. I stopped by the front window. Outside its colonial panes, in the dusk and rain,
three figures waited. For what? I turned back to
Mackenzie and caught him in midyawn.

"'Scuse me," he said. "You were searching for a
phone?"

"It took a long time. Everybody was still at work.
Then I found Mrs. Steinman. I was leaving her door,
too, because nobody answered. But she's on a walker,
so it took her a while. Then I had to explain without
scaring her, and she's hard of hearing, so it was slow.
And even then, she didn't want to let me in."

"But you did eventually phone from the Steinman
house."

"Danzig. It's the Danzigs' house. Mrs. Steinman is Elaine Danzig's mother. Lives with them ever since she broke her hip. That was about seven months ago."

His eyes were closing all the way.

"Sorry. Well. I guess I've said it all. That's where I called, and I waited there for the police to arrive. Then we came here, and that's it."

He didn't say anything, just slowly heaved himself out of the chair and meandered around. "Yay-uss," he began, "but not quite all of it." He reached the kitchen area. "Why did you then try to clean things away in here?" He stared at me from behind the counter-divider.

My cheeks heated up. In ninth grade, somebody told me I would lose my blush when I lost my virginity. Somebody lied.

"Miss Peppah," he insisted. "Why?"

I shrugged.

He walked over to me. "We're talkin' about the scene of a crime."

"It was a reflex," I whispered.

All he did was lift an eyebrow, but I felt as if he'd tightened the screws on the rack. "It's my mother, you see. There was cat food and sugar and coffee, and there were police all over the place, and a photographer, a camera, for God's sake...."

Even I was having trouble believing I'd been such a complete fool as to whip out a broom while a battalion of men were painstakingly collecting evidence. "Listen," I said, with forced casualness, "I didn't want it seen, you know?"

"Evidence of a struggle?" he murmured. "What made you wait so long, though? I mean before you left the house, you could have—"

"No struggle! It was just the camera, that police photographer." My cheeks were scalding. I took a deep breath and plunged into humiliating honesty. "I regressed. Listen, when I was a kid, my mother convinced me that if I ever wore torn underwear and I was in an accident, the surgeons wouldn't bother saving me, and the rest of the family would die of shame. This afternoon, well, it seemed very important to tidy up."

"Gotcha," he said, and he actually grinned, showing a lot of very white teeth. He walked away a pace or two. "You smoke?" he asked abruptly.

"Well, actually, I haven't yet today, but sure, I'd love one." I could always stop another, less stressful day.

But the only thing he pulled out was a ratty brown notebook. "Ashtray's full," he said. "All one brand."

"Liza smoked," I said.

He nodded. "Anything missing from the house?"

"Nothing I can see. Except my cat. I told the others —I can't find him. I think he got out when whoever..." I pushed the image away.

"Give it some time. Cats come back," he said. "Nothing else, though?"

I shrugged. "I haven't checked everywhere yet. The others told me not to touch anything."

"Proceed to touch. Doesn't look like a robbery, anyway. The obvious stuff is still here—TV, stereo. All neat and tidy. Tell your mother I said so."

We methodically checked through the cupboards and drawers on the first floor. All I can say is that having your drawers examined is as embarrassing as it sounds, and deserves advance warning. I felt especially mortified when my jelly-jar drinking glasses were exposed to his silent scrutiny.

Of course, nothing was missing. Even thieves have standards.

Then we faced the staircase. I knew the other men

had checked the house, but I couldn't lose the feeling that something still lurked behind a drape, inside a closet. I followed Mackenzie up the steps reluctantly.

At the bedroom door, Mackenzie lifted one eyebrow again.

I shook my head. "I left it that way, unmade," I said. I would have again explained, unnecessarily, about Liza's arrival, except I couldn't bear thinking her name, let alone saying it. "What would anybody want to steal up here?" I asked. "I don't have furs."

"Tape recorders? Jewelry?"

I pawed through the leather box on my dresser. Would even a drug-crazed lunatic covet Jimmy Petrus's junior varsity basketball charm? Or my National Honor Society pin? I was heavy on sentiment, low on cash value.

"There's nothing on the third floor worth taking," I said, "unless somebody's desperate for lesson plans." But I was glad he insisted on inspecting it, and I followed him up and stood back as he surveyed my messy desk in one of the two small rooms at the top. He picked up an ancient blurry stencil and read:

> "'Sad is my spirit and sore it grieves me
> To tell to any the trouble and shame
> That Grendel hath brought me with bitter hate. . . .'"

"*Beowulf*," he said, putting the sheet down. His back was toward me, but I nodded. "Used to love that poem. Probably directed me toward police work, although his methodology was somewhat primitive, ripping people's arms off and such. But effective. Stopped a crime wave." He pronounced the word "crahm" and gave it a certain charm.

He looked up at the wall. "How's that part go now? Ah, yes:

> "'But always the mead hall, the morning after
> The splendid building, was blood bespattered:
> Daylight dawned on the drippings of swords. . . .'"

"Great stuff," he added, turning to me. He grinned and I tried, a second too late, to look nonchalant about his literacy.

"Surprised because I'm Southern, or because I'm a cop?" he asked, always yawning through his words. "Which stereotype got ya?"

I clamped my mouth shut.

He grinned. "Ah have known some great English teachers," he said softly, ushering me out of the room.

The last room is my storehouse. It has a folded rollaway cot and cartons full of clothing I'm sure will come back into style. It also had something making noise inside the closet.

I strangled my scream.

Mackenzie stood beside the closet door and whipped it open.

One nervous cat scampered out.

"Macavity! I've been so worried!" I scooped him into my arms. "He's old," I explained, stroking his salt-and-pepper fur. "Must be really upset, poor thing. I'll bet he was closed in by the police who were inspecting the room. Accidentally," I added for Mackenzie's sake.

"Macavity?" the detective said, poking around the cartons. "So you've seen *Cats*, too."

"No. I, well, yes, but I named him before that." I didn't know why I felt compelled to continue, but I did. "From the poems." I wasn't going to let an arrogant cop who remembered *Beowulf* question my credentials.

"Ah," he said sympathetically. "And then came the hit show, and now ever'body knows about T. S. Eliot's mystery cat, and your pet's name doesn't prove you're better read than anybody else." He shook his head. "Might as well put the animal to sleep, don't you think?"

I watched the smart-ass cop turn out the light to the storeroom, and I followed him down the stairs. At the bottom, he looked around. "So it wasn't robbery," he said. "Never thought it was. She was wearing a nifty diamond ring, if you recall."

I didn't care. I suddenly felt ready to collapse. Even my ears drooped.

"No sign of struggle, if your floor-cleaning story is true. Just the hit on that fireplace stone. Pretty forceful one, I'd say. The lab reports will tell us if the hair and blood are hers." I shuddered. He ignored me and continued his soliloquy. "So. What do we have?" he asked himself.

"Mackenzie? I want to leave now, please? I have to get away from here."

He watched me for a moment. "Your fastidious mama, is she nearby?"

"Florida. I have a sister in Gladwyne, though."

"Fine. But first tell me about Liza Nichols." He was better at poetry than compassion.

"I worked with her. I don't know her."

"But she came callin' at 8:00 A.M. on a rainy Monday?"

"It surprised me, too. But it seemed accidental—she was near here; it was miserable out, so she came. Anyway, I didn't have time to probe reasons. I had to get to school."

"Why didn't she?"

"She was an actress trying to put together a stake so she could move to New York. So she moved back in with her mother, did modeling, and taught drama an hour or two a day."

"New York? But you told that first policeman she was engaged to Hayden Cole."

"Now she is. She only met him in February. She changed plans, but she was finishing out her contract at school and still doing a little modeling."

"She was engaged to Cole after two months?"

"Whirlwind courtship. They were supposed to be married three weeks from now. Right before the May primary. Listen, Mackenzie, I'm wiped out. Let me pack and call my sister, okay?"

"Soon," he said. "She from old money, like the Coles?"

I shook my head. "No money." I shuffled over to the staircase and leaned against the newel post. "I feel awful."

He looked at me sternly.

Now I felt guilty, too. How could I complain about my weariness, about how dreadful I felt when Liza . . . I clamped down again to stop the thick, dizzy terror that her memory provoked. I could discuss her dispassionately, but I couldn't think about her.

"Background," he said.

"I don't know what happened to her father. But her mother worked as a baby-sitter, a sort of nanny, since Liza was little. That's all I know. I was in Liza's house only once, when I dropped her off after school. Neither she nor her mother blurted out their life stories during that visit. Can I call my sister now?"

"Strange match," he said. "You know the Coles?"

I know defeat. I sat down on the bottom step,

yawned without covering my mouth and shook my head.

"Know about them, then?"

I shrugged.

"Can you be a little more informative, Miss Peppah?" His drawl increased with his annoyance. "I'm not from these parts, y'know."

"I surmised. That's not your basic Philadelphia accent."

"Good. All of you sound like you have sinus problems."

"We do."

"So I'd 'preciate background. Anything. Raymond, my partner, is a native Philadelphian, but he claims to know nothing about what he calls 'those people.'"

I took a deep breath and tried to remember everything Liza had ever told me. The newspapers were more discreet about the Coles, playing down their baronial splendors. "I don't know about 'those people,' either. They were snatching up prime U.S. real estate while my ancestors were still convinced the earth was flat. His mother's old New England shipping money. And his father's family goes back before the Civil War, maybe the Revolution. Coles had land grants. Coles built our banks and schools. Coles helped finance the Main Line, the real main line of the railroad. And then they settled on the right side of the tracks and counted their money. I guess when there was enough, they decided to start running the state. Now, is that enough?"

"You were at their house for the engagement party. Where is it? Ray's lookin' it up, but—"

"I hope not in the phone book, where it will not be. It's in Ardmore, up a winding road on top of a hill. Has some cutesy name, not a number out front. You can't miss it. It sprawls all over a hilltop. Has the columns of tall trees for the carriages to pass through. An entry hall twice the size of this house. Lovely, as long as you have a dozen servants to tidy up. They do. That's all I know. They hate publicity, anything flashy, and money that's inadequate or of the wrong vintage. And you could have gotten everything I said out of *Who's Who*."

"Then tell me what I can't get from a book."

I was learning about Southern men. Their sharp edges lay buried under those sweet blurred consonants. Until they cut you.

"Come on, Miss Pepper. You've had a shock, but you're strong. Tell me what Cole is like."

"I met him only that once, at the party. He was very genial. Very cordial."

"And? You have some impression of him?"

"It's probably wrong, or unfair. I was overwhelmed by the scale of the place. Maybe that's why his kindness offended me. I felt he was granting me an audience, that I wasn't real to him. I was one of his fiancée's friends, part of a package that would be dropped after the wedding. Or the election."

"Did he do anything in particular to make you feel that way?"

I shook my head. "He did only the right things. Maybe that's what was wrong. And I have to say, I don't think somebody who makes you feel that way—ordinary, unimportant—is much of a political candidate. I think at heart he's sorry this is a democracy."

Mackenzie raked his fingers through his hair. It bounced back to its original crinkles and twists. "Do you know what was bothering Liza Nichols?"

"No. Didn't I already tell you that? I don't even know if anything really was. She was an actress. She loved to work over an audience for the sport of it."

"You didn't like her much, did you?"

"Please. I'm so tired. I don't know that answer."

"That's all, then." He gestured toward the street. "The media's still out there, cultivatin' pneumonia. I'll get you through. I'll even drive you to that parking lot of yours. Raymond should be back at the car by now. Go get your toothbrush."

I started up the stairs.

"Call these Trinity houses, don't they?" he said, and I nodded. "Yeah, Raymond told me. Three little floors —Father, Son, and Holy Ghost. Although that doesn't make much sense. Raymond says these used to be servants' quarters. His folks lived near here. Then the city did some urban removal—"

"Renewal."

"Not for Raymond's family. Houses were painted and prettied and priced out. And in came people like you."

"Just what does that mean? You don't know what I'm like."

He grinned and shrugged. "Observations at the scene of the crahm. Want to hear?"

"Does it matter?"

He stood up and walked around as he spoke, like a lawyer presenting his case to the jury. "This house is a perch, not a nest. A good address—not a real flighty single's place—not a *desperate* place, you know? But still portable. Open to changes of heart and chance." He grinned up at me. The little pilot light in my cheeks ignited.

"Exhibit one, the suede chair. The single, irresistible long-term investment. Exhibit two, jelly jars for solitary juice drinking versus cut crystal for guests. The reupholstered sofa. Back to Granny's attic someday, without a twinge. But, over it, decent graphics that can be packed in a flash. Exhibit three, the practical, but not overdone bedroom. No head board. Just handsome linens and a frame—again, movable, adjustable. And not that settled-in spinster kind who lives in the bedroom. Desk is somewhere else, and I didn' see evidence that you'd had Sunday night dinner up there in bed, either. Exhibit four—you've got a coffee bean grinder in the cupboard, and beans in the freezer, but you were drinkin' and spillin' instant this mornin'. Beans are contingency fare. Like the good wine in the pantry versus the jug wine in the fridge. So...tenant is happy enough, but worried about gettin' too happy all on her own, so she's ready, but not particularly willing, to cut and run. Because she's also hoping some adventure is going to happen upon her, make things change. Fairly mixed-up type. Fairly typical. Am I right? Don't answer. I know I am."

There was enough truth, and arrogance, in what he'd said to make me furious.

"Yay-uss," he said. "Concern for appearance, to be sure, although you don't like thinkin' you care about savin' face. But good address, good chair, good crystal, good wine. And lots else is makin' do. Now go pack," he said paternally. "I'll bet the suitcase is a good one. That can move with you. Wherever. Oh, yay-uss. Write down your sister's address. And you'll be at school tomorrow, won't you?"

"Mackenzie," I said slowly, "why do you need to know my future locales? I was hoping this meeting, however sweet, would be our last."

"Come on now, Amanda Pepper. Don't take it personally. On an off day, when you aren't scanning *Beowulf*, don't you ever sneak in a whodunit? Don't you know standard cop prose? The old 'don't leave town without notifying me' number?" He turned and looked out the dark window facing the narrow street.

I marched up to my not-exactly-permanent bed-room, suddenly empathizing with people who called cops "pigs."

Three

MY SISTER'S HOUSE WAS TWENTY MINUTES and a world away, insulated from the sirens and shouts of the city by a greenbelt circling its western edge. As I walked up the forsythia-lined path from Beth's driveway, I heard only the rain and my own footsteps.

"Mandy!" My hand was still on the bell when she pulled me into her house. "I've been so worried since you called!"

I reassured her that I was fine. And I began to believe it. The grandfather clock was ticking calmly, eternally denying the possibility of shock and evil mischance. There were hothouse flowers on the hall table and a domestic tableau in the living room that was as comforting as the end of a fairy tale. It was impossible to envision violence in a house such as this.

"I held off my appointment until you got here," my brother-in-law said, rising from his wing chair and kissing me lightly.

I like Sam too much to call him plodding or phlegmatic. But for Sam, a man as regular as the clapper of the grandfather clock, delaying an appointment is tantamount to hysteria.

"Mommy let me stay up," my niece, Karen, said. She flew at me, and we did some heavy hugging.

Even the family dog, Horse, staggered over and licked my hand.

"All right, everybody. Amanda's here now, so it's up to bed, Karen," Beth said.

Karen pouted, protested, inadvertently yawned, and finally agreed to go upstairs if I came and tucked her in shortly.

"Now. What happened?" Beth asked the moment her daughter was out of earshot.

"Why don't we feed the poor girl while you interrogate her?" Sam asked mildly.

"I hope the chicken isn't dried out," Beth said, handing me a platter.

It wasn't. Beth's house is well over a hundred years old, but she doesn't live in the past. The fireplace in the kitchen warms the heart; the microwave rewarms the food. I told my story, again gliding over the parts I couldn't bear replaying. The difference was that Sam and Beth, unlike the police, didn't want graphic details, so the telling became almost routine and smooth. "I think they suspect me," I said in conclusion.

Sam clucked. "That's your imagination. And if so, then as soon as they know more, they'll crawl to your doorstep and beg forgiveness."

I had a hard time envisioning C. K. Mackenzie either crawling or begging.

"Poor Hayden," Beth murmured. She picked up my plate, gesturing for me to stay put. "What a mess this will be with the Cole family involved."

"Do you know him?" I asked.

"Barely," Sam answered. "Knew him years ago, my freshman year at Franklin and Marshall. He was a junior. I was a pledge in his fraternity. But he transferred to Penn that spring. Now we're on some of the same committees, legal associations. That's all." He stood up. "I really must keep that appointment now. Try to relax, Mandy."

Beth walked him to the door, then came back and poured two cups of coffee. "Sam won't gossip," she said with an imitation pout. "If he knew anything, he wouldn't say it until he checked it out for possible libel suits. He thinks in small print." Those traits didn't seem to bother her one whit. "Anyway," she continued, "you probably know Hayden better through Liza than we do."

"She never said much about him. Just that he was a proper gentleman of the old school. Behaved in a manner that would please Queen Victoria. I always figured she meant he was boring as hell. I don't even know how much she cared about him. I remember, right after she got her engagement ring, she said, 'A smart person never lets emotions interfere with her life.' The thing is, I don't know if those were her real feelings, a quote from something, or what. She sometimes fell into a Noël Coward mode, all clipped sentences and emotions."

"Or maybe she was trying to fit into Hayden's world," Beth said. "He didn't seem at all emotional. At least, not in public. Family trait, from what I've seen. I worked on a hospital committee with his mother. A neighbor, Sissie, roped me into it. And Mrs. Cole's the same reserved, steely type. Typical old Main Line, you know?"

"Who's Sissie?" I asked. I had heard that name before, but the day's events had jangled my mental connectors and robbed the memory bank.

"Letitia Abbott Bellinger, but nobody calls her that. She lives down the street. We carpool. Why?"

The name clicked into place. Gus had mentioned her. "She's involved in the Playhouse, I think. The one Liza..."

Beth, always gentle, always sensitive, helped me across the name. "She's into a hundred things. Little theater, the Museum Council, local politics, hospital charities. She's at loose ends. Divorcing Mr. Bellinger isn't a full-time occupation, although it's been going on long enough. She's always been close with Hayden. In fact, I heard it was once assumed they would marry, but then she surprised everybody with Bellinger."

Karen padded into the kitchen in pink-footed pajamas. "I waited and *waited*," she said. "Read to me?" She held a copy of *Winnie the Pooh*. I didn't feel capable of working a chubby bear into this particular day.

"Aunt Mandy's too tired," Beth said. "I think she's going to fall asleep before you do."

"Then will you tuck me in?" Karen asked. The girl was only in nursery school, but with her gene pool, she was destined to be a pragmatic bargainer. I capitulated and staggered upstairs.

When I descended again, the grandfather clock was chiming. I looked at it and felt as if I had gone through a time warp. It was only eight-thirty.

"In here," Beth called from the living room.

For a while we both stared at the softly burning fire in the grate.

"So," she said after a while, "what's been happening?"

"Been happening?" My mouth fell open. "Beth!"

"Besides that."

I grinned in spite of myself. Corpses were trivial, fleeting items. Men were forever. "I broke up with Donald," I answered. Beth would be pleased. His emerald eyes had never blinded her to his innumerable personality flaws, and she had become exasperated with our long, drawn-out, dithering miseries. "Also with cigarettes."

"I wonder if you'll ever settle down," she murmured. The five-year difference between us made her consider herself my mentor, and since our bona fide mother's relocation left a vacuum, Beth, like nature, whooshed in to fill the void.

"What could be more settled than a schoolteacher who lives with a cat?"

"You manage to meet the most impossible assortment of males imaginable, have more complications and more problems—and now look what's happened to you!"

"Let me get this straight. You think I should get married because somebody...died in my living room?" I settled more deeply into the sofa cushions, admiring the extremes my family will go to in search of a rationale to end my single state.

"Ah, well," Beth said almost wistfully. "Maybe I'm just a lousy role model. Scaring you away with nightmares of carpools and volunteer work. Suburban clichés."

Every revolution has victims, and Beth was definitely a casualty of the Women's Movement. She had been born knowing what she wanted to do with her life, and she was doing it—loving, nurturing, helping.

In other eras, she would have been the subject of epic poems. Freud would have crowned her as the epitome of healthy womanhood. But today, Beth was depressed because she was happy at home, because her ambitions were traditional and inadequate for the contemporary heroine.

During the great Coca-Cola switch-over, I tried to tell Beth to think of herself as the Classic form, to realize that she, like Coke, didn't have to reinvent herself. But she didn't see the connection.

The doorbell rang. I looked at my watch, ready to be outraged by midnight callers. But it still wasn't late anyplace except in my head.

Beth left the room, and after the front door clicked, I heard the sharp rise and fall of a woman's voice.

"I saw the six o'clock news," it said, "about Hayden's —about Liza, and then the name of the girl whose house—and I said to my housekeeper, 'Why that's Beth Wyman's sister. I met her at the engagement party. At least I think it is.' Is it? They showed a picture of her leaving her house, but I couldn't really tell. Is it? Wasn't your maiden name Pepper? I'm sure your sister is that Amanda, isn't she?"

Maybe Beth was nodding agreement. She certainly wasn't getting a chance to fit a word in. The other voice billowed and waved, up and down a vocal roller coaster, one sound sliding into the next. She filled the house with nervous energy, and I disliked her without knowing who she was.

"What a horrible thing for Hayden," she continued. "How awful for anyone to have to find. Was your sister close with Liza? The news really said nothing. It's dreadful, isn't it?" She stopped to inhale, or take more drugs, or whatever it was that kept her in constant motion.

Beth seized the moment. "Sissie, Mandy's here. Come see her. Let me take your coat and umbrella."

Sissie Bellinger was beige. She walked into the living room in a café au lait silk blouse and tailored brown slacks. Her ash-blond hair framed a pale, fine-featured face. In her mid-thirties, she was not yet deeply into Main Line dowdiness. Right now, she had somewhat worn but classic good looks.

"I shouldn't stay," she said, settling nonetheless on the pale green love seat. "Should be at the Playhouse, but I saw the news, and what are we going to do now? The place will be a madhouse, total confusion. Thank God we only do shows on weekends, but what should we do? Cancel? Does the show go on anyway?"

I opened my mouth, ready to say hello or to try to answer her barrage of questions, but she continued on, looking earnest and agitated.

"Liza's the lead, for God's sake." She stood up, paced while she spoke, until she found a crystal ashtray. Its tiny size might have been a clue as to Beth's feelings about smoking in the house, but it escaped Sissie's notice. She sat down again, lit up, and brushed smoke away as she spoke. "This is the most shocking—who could have predicted?"

"Coffee, Sissie?" Beth asked. "I have some ready."

Sissie waved her slender wrist in front of her eyes. There was a gold watch on it, but she didn't read it. "I should leave," she said. "But no point yet. Just hysteria waiting. Yes, I'd love some."

It was certainly easy making conversation with this woman. You didn't even have to know the native tongue.

"I'll be right back," Beth said.

Sissie took that as a signal finally to communicate with me. In her fashion. "So you, poor thing, became involved in Liza's—" She had pale brown eyes that flicked over my face several times. "Was it awful?"

"It was—"

"Do they, the police, know who did it? The television said nothing, but of course they'd never say, all those libel laws and interference by the press and things."

I wasn't sure if that had been a question until Sissie puffed and waved smoke away, clearing airtime for me.

"It had only just happened when I—"

"When?" Sissie stubbed out the cigarette. "When did it happen? Do they know? Was anyone seen? I suppose they questioned the neighbors. Why was she at your house?"

C. K. Mackenzie was easier to take than this interrogator. I felt battered and slow-witted as I sifted through her questions, deciding that I had no obligation to answer them, even if she'd let me.

"I just know everybody will be talking about it at the Playhouse, you see." She lit another cigarette. I thought about the full ashtray in my living room and tried to see what brand she smoked. Her brown leather case hid the package, so I gave up playing detective for the time being.

"Was she your roommate?" Sissie's lids lowered. "She said she lived with her mother." Her cultivated voice was heavy with malice and insinuation.

"She was visiting."

Beth returned and busied herself with coffee cups and cookies. "You knew Liza, didn't you, Sissie?" she asked.

Sissie looked offended. "Well, not really." The question silenced her momentarily.

"What did you think of her?" I asked in what I hoped was a sweet, somewhat indifferent voice. It felt great being the asker of questions for a change.

Sissie sighed. "What can I say? She's gone now." She looked toward the ceiling for heavenly guidance, but opted to proceed without it. "I'm a frank, straightforward person. Isn't that right, Beth?"

There was a tiny pause, a missed beat.

She was an insane, rich person. Rich enough so that her behavior was probably relabeled "eccentric."

"So, while I hate to speak ill of the dead, I see no

reason suddenly to become a hypocrite." She paused while the hall clock chimed the hour. "Oh, I'll be late; they'll be angry. They depend on me so much."

Only once in all the years that Gus had been associated with the Playhouse had he mentioned, politely, Sissie Bellinger's name, and never his dependence on her.

"Liza was common," she announced. "Anyone with a mind could see that no good would come of that match. He never wanted to marry her anyway."

"What do you mean?" My loud voice, crashing through her barrage of words, was probably also common.

"Mean? Well, I suppose he wanted to, but only because he hadn't time to know her. She was a good actress, you know. I'll give her that. He never saw what she was really like. I tried to warn him, but, well...and she! Such an inflated idea of who she was! Such a temper!" She crossed her legs and pursed her lips with distaste.

"When did you see her last?" I asked.

"Last night." Sissie's eyes became slits, and she paused, holding a cigarette heavy with ash. "Why? What did she tell you?" she asked.

"Nothing," I answered quickly, but Sissie stayed frozen in place. "I teach with Gus Winston. He said Liza was angry last night, after the show. When you mentioned her temper, remembering her that way, I thought—"

"No," she said, finally flicking her ash. "I saw her at dinner. With Hayden, before the show. Hayden had to leave to give a speech. I drove Liza to the Playhouse." She ground out the cigarette. The ashtray now overflowed, and there were gray flecks of ash on the polished mahogany end table. "Then I left," Sissie

continued, as if establishing an alibi. "The police have
no leads, is that it?"

"None that I know of."

"Well, then." She stood up. "Lovely meeting you
again, Amanda." She went into the hallway and Beth
followed.

"She isn't real," I said when my sister returned. "Is
she always like that?"

Beth nodded. "I don't go out of my way to see her.
We carpool, see each other on committees, things like
that. She has never dropped over before. Awful, isn't
she? Wreaking havoc, hurting people, calling it frank-
ness. Even at nursery school, she's caused more trouble. . . ."

"Do you think she's in love with Hayden Cole?" I
asked.

"I don't think she's ever been in love with anybody
but herself. But I know she's not in love with being
single again. Maybe she resents Hayden's marrying
someone else when she's reentering the market."

I walked over to the ashtray next to the love seat.
The stubs in it were the same low-tar brand as Liza's.
"Tell me, Beth," I said softly. "Do you think she re-
sented it enough to beat his bride-to-be's head against
my fireplace wall?"

Four

SUNSHINE, EXOTIC AND DELICIOUS, WOKE ME up. The sky through the window was freshly laundered and glowing. Someone should write a song about great days in Philadelphia. Three songs. One for each of them.

Up the stairs came morning sounds, home sounds. Dishes chinking, soft voices. I dressed and went to meet them. By the time I reached the kitchen, I felt almost good about life. Last night's fitful sleep and predawn insomnia didn't matter. Yesterday was now officially over. It couldn't be undone, but it could be cleaned up and away, following nature's example.

"Good morning!" Beth said with surprise. "But I wanted you to sleep late."

"Can't, Beth. I have to go to school. The kids are going to be upset. Maybe I can help them through it a little."

Beth pursed her mouth, but she handed me coffee instead of advice, and I thanked her on both counts.

Karen, wearing a train conductor's blue striped overalls, came in dragging my pocketbook behind her. She handed it to me, then stood there, looking expectant and pleased.

"Is there something I'm forgetting?" I asked.

"I found it," Karen said, breaking into giggles. "I found it and I like it. Thank you." And from behind her back, she brought a crumple of brown paper cradling a red plush jeweler's box.

"What were you doing in Aunt Mandy's purse?" Beth asked sternly. "What did you take?" She put her hand out.

"I was getting it for her. The box...it sort of fell out." Nonetheless, Karen reluctantly passed it and its wrapping paper to her mother.

"This is addressed to Liza," Beth said softly.

"Good Lord. I forgot all about it. I thought it was some kind of sample, anyway. Like toothpaste or minipads. It was in Liza's mailbox at school."

"This was in it, too," Karen said, producing a receipt. "Is this a card? Does it say me? I can't read writing."

But the delicate tracery spelled out the name of a jewelry shop downtown. One of my favorites, in front of which I have spent happy moments daydreaming. I do have aspirations beyond Jimmy Petrus's J.V. football. This jeweler is famous for his whimsical creations. The bill in my hand was for five hundred dollars, a modest sum for his sense of humor.

Inside the plush box, a charm was suspended from a heavy chain. Both were very gold.

"You see?" Karen said, "it's for me." She reached toward the charm, a tiny bear clutching an even more minuscule bucket in his paw.

"Sweetheart, it isn't mine, or I'd give it to you," I said. "Anyway, it doesn't seem meant for a child."

"But it's Winnie the Pooh," Karen logically insisted.

On his tiny bucket, delicate tracery spelled out "Happy Birthday, Honey."

I dangled the chain in front of her. "Look, it reaches your belly-button. It wouldn't fit you."

"Then whose is it?" Karen said in a sulky voice. "Who does it fit?"

"I can't imagine," I said honestly.

Twice I checked to be sure my car was locked before I headed around toward the school door. I walked slowly, trying to savor the sunshine, trying to delay my entry into a building filled with questions waiting to be asked.

"Hey! You!" The voice was almost as heavy and frightening as the sudden hand on my shoulder.

I pulled away and backed off, ready to use—if I could only remember it—my one-day self-defense seminar. All I instantly recalled was the gouging-out-of-eyes part, which seemed excessive as a first response. Anyway, it was morning, and we were in a high school parking lot—a ridiculous time and place for a mugging.

I ran three steps. The enormous man shouted. "Wait! You! Wait!" He managed to be at my side in about one stride, his bulk casting a shadow over me.

"Are you out of your mind?" I broke into a run, aiming for the front of the building, where there would be safety in numbers. Our students never rushed inside, eager to beat the bell. But the alleyway was narrow, and the man caught hold of me as I swung left. This time he didn't let go, although I struggled. He tugged and pulled me back, toward an oversized black car idling at the alley curb.

Every organized crime cliché packed my head so tightly I couldn't think. I was frozen, staring at the black limousine. Another figure sat behind the tinted glass.

"Let me go!" I screamed as he opened the back door of the car. And then I remembered. I stopped tugging, wheeled on the monster, and aimed my knee straight up. That lesson was compliments of my original self-defense instructor, Mama, who had coughed and blushed and finally just spelled out what to do in desperate situations. I believe she meant something other than being dragged into a criminal's car, but I didn't care.

My molester grunted and doubled over, still clutching my arm.

"Haskell!" a voice from inside the car said. "You're hurting her."

Haskell, looking like a hunchback, didn't inform the voice that I had evened the score. Instead, he dropped my arm.

"Miss Pepper!" the voice called.

I waited. Haskell wouldn't be racing after me for a while, and the voice sounded strangely familiar. "Mr. Cole?" I asked when the tinted glass rolled down.

"Just a minute of your time, please," he said calmly. "I apologize for Haskell's methods. I didn't mean for him to frighten you." He glared at the beefy man; then he looked at his watch. "Miss Pepper, can I have five minutes? We'll just ride around, and you'll be back in time for class." He opened the car door wider.

My mother had told me all about cars and strange men, and Hayden Cole seemed very strange. I shook my head.

"Now, Miss Pepper. I am not an old man offering candy," he said, annoyed. I felt ashamed, as if he'd read my thoughts. "Five minutes?"

A sliver of normal, nonparanoid perception returned. Hayden Cole was not exactly the Godfather. I got into the car. "Five minutes," I said.

"Once again I apologize for Haskell's behavior." He paused and seemed to consider things. "And mine," he finally added.

"What is it you want?"

I looked at his profile, contained and still. Less than twenty-four hours earlier, the man's bride-to-be had been smashed to death. I couldn't see any evidence of heavy mourning, but perhaps I didn't understand good breeding.

The car circled the general area of the school, slowly going nowhere. I waited for an explanation. I waited quite a while. My tension level increased with each second of silence.

He blinked a few times; then he took a thin cigar out of a case, clipped off the end, and bit it. Smoking cigars does not seem politically wise. Neither was it particularly pleasant in a car in the morning, even to a smoke-starved woman such as I. I waved at the air. He ignored me.

I wondered if he had dragged me into his car just for the pleasure of snubbing me.

His hand holding the cigar shook slightly, and his strong profile melted down a bit, blurred. Still studying his cigar, he finally spoke. "I have to know about... about Liza." He seemed unable to turn his head and face me, and I almost, for a moment, felt a wave of pity for him.

"I have to know—I couldn't wait until you finished teaching. The police were so uninformative...." He lit another match and let it burn down to his fingertips before he realized it and blew it out. Then he noticed that he didn't need a light at all, but he kept staring at the cigar. He was not the man I'd described to Mackenzie, and I mentally apologized for not considering him a mourner. Even his voice had changed. It was muffled, unsure, fumbling.

"I'm not sure I can help you," I said softly.

He finally looked at me, and the pity I had been developing atrophied and disappeared. "You have to," he said, his voice steely again. "You can. You were there. She was in your house, after all. You know a great deal."

Distraught. The man is distraught, I told myself. Maybe he never learned to express himself graciously. Maybe he had bad English teachers. Or maybe he's really in pain. You're not hearing threats, you're hearing a different style. His conception of his divine rights. He doesn't know any better. Sometimes even rich folks need charity, Amanda.

"Mr. Cole, I'll tell you whatever I know, but I'm afraid it doesn't amount to much."

"But you knew her. She spent so much time with you."

"Come on, you and I know—" I stopped myself. She had used me as a cover-up, but for whom? Not, I suddenly, fully, realized for long nights of passion with Hayden Cole. "—how little time there really is, after all the work, the paper marking, the cleaning up, is done." I knew I was babbling, and so did he, but he didn't know it was to protect his male ego.

"I have to know what happened," he said, his eyes like storm clouds. "What did she say to you? Why was she at your house? What did she say?"

I shook my head and glanced at my watch. "I think our five minutes are just about—"

He exhaled loudly. "Surely she told you something. *Something!*"

"I wish she had."

He clenched his jaw around the cigar, and I saw a vein near his temple surface and throb. Distraught, I reminded myself again, but, oh, how I wished he would say something about Liza. About how he missed her, or couldn't bear not knowing who had done such a hideous thing. "Listen, Mr. Cole," I prompted him, "I understand how terrible this must be for you—"

He stiffened, rejecting the idea that I could understand him in any way, so I rushed on. "And I wish I could tell you something definite, but I can't."

"The way she was—how did she—what did the police say to you?"

I lowered my window discreetly and watched his smoke float by. Why did he seem so much the tense interrogator, so little the bereaved?

"Miss Pepper, what did they say?"

"They think she was pushed against the fireplace. The wall is stone, a rough finish. They don't think it was an accident. Too much force, too much impact, for one thing. I'm sure they told you the same thing."

"But any clues as to who might have done it?"

I felt as if a frigid wind were blowing off him. I pulled back and shook my head. "I'll be late. Tell the driver..."

He bit his bottom lip, nodded, and tapped the glass. We headed back toward the school. I busied myself with ignoring the man beside me.

"Miss Pepper," he said as Haskell put the car into park and opened his door, "did she say anything, anything at all, about me? About...the future? About... plans?" His voice was hoarse, his face lined and sallow.

I had the sense that several different men had been riding beside me in the past five minutes.

"No," I said softly. "No."

Hayden Cole sat back against the wine-dark upholstery. "I see," he said quietly.

The interview was over. Haskell held open my door and kept his face impassive as I left. I didn't bid either man farewell.

I felt light-headed and disoriented as I checked in at the office.

"Miss Pepper?" Dr. Havermeyer was nervous, unlike himself. I turned to my leader, my headmaster. He patted his stomach, absently smoothing his vest. He coughed and moved two steps closer, close enough so I could study a tiny shaving nick on one of his chins. "We thought you might want the day off, to..." He seemed unable to complete the sentence. Even with the imperial "we" he was stymied, stuck, searching for the precise circumlocution. "In light of the difficult time you are experiencing, we thought..."

"I'm fine," I said quickly.

His troubled expression didn't clear. "Well, but after the, ah, and the press, and the photographers, we, ah, the school image, of course. Naturally, we stand behind you, no implications, no hidden agenda, of course, but..."

I stood my ground, refusing to pick up any of his unsavory droppings.

"Well," he said, fumbling with the key he always wore, a key that resembled, but was not from, Phi Beta Kappa. "Yes. Of course. So many telephone calls this morning. Indeed. Well, we must hope this terrible incident is cleared up quickly, mustn't we?"

I said we must, and interpreting his renewed tummy rub as dismissal, I left the office.

Gus was on his way in, but he stopped in his tracks when he saw me. "What happened?" he said. "I heard it from Sissie at the Playhouse. What happened?"

"Everybody keeps asking me, and I don't know."

He gripped my arm much too tightly. The same one Haskell had already abused. "Who do they think killed her?"

"You're hurting me!"

He stared at me, then at his hand before letting go.

"I can't believe it," he said. He pulled a newspaper out of his attaché case and punched at it. "I cannot—"

Terrific. I was page-one news. There was a snap of Liza, a handsome portrait of Hayden Cole, and, above a subheading, "Body Found in Center-City House," a photo that immortalized my exit last night. Mackenzie didn't look half bad, but I was stooped over, my raincoat pulled up high because I'd lost my rain hat somewhere, my hand half shielding my face. All in all, a sterling impersonation of a felon avoiding the paparazzi.

"No wonder Havermeyer's blithering," I murmured. "I wouldn't want that woman to teach my children, either." I felt suddenly afraid. "What am I going to do? They suspect me."

Gus blinked a few times, getting me back in focus. "Ridiculous," he said, "but is there something I can do to help?"

"You could have been visible after school," I said. "To back my alibi. They found it hard to believe I hung around here for no reason."

"I was in the bookroom!" His voice was too forceful for an intimate twosome.

"Don't get defensive. I'm the only one who needs the alibi."

I hoped, for Gus's sake, that I was telling the truth.

Liza had dramatically enriched my first-period class two whole months ago. Maybe she was a dim memory to most of the students, because they seemed excited, not upset. They passed around copies of the newspaper, and I flinched each time I saw my photograph whiz by.

Only Stacy Felkin was beside herself with grief. And no wonder. The moment Liza had entered the classroom, Stacy of the limp hair, the thick waist, had found her heroine and model. She imprinted Liza on her brain like a duckling, imitating, best as she could, each and every gesture and mannerism of her idol.

Liza had style. Stacy, reproducing it, had pathos. For months now, Stacy walked with a slow swish of lumpy hips, flicking back lank dirty-blond hair, smiling mysteriously. She was an inflated, porous imitation of the real thing, the Wonder Bread of sex. Even so, high school boys produce too many hormones to be overly critical.

Today Stacy wasn't into seductiveness. She was thoroughly, decisively, into misery. Her mascara had smeared into raccoon eyes, her nose was swollen and her lipstick chewed off. She clutched a box of tissues.

If ever there was a time for me to offer aid and comfort, this seemed it. I put my hand on her shoulder. She blew her nose into a lilac tissue. "Oh," she wailed, "isn't this the worst thing that ever happened?" The room around us became very silent. Almost respectful, I thought.

"Death is always terrible," I said quietly. "And when it's unexpected and violent, it's even worse." I could hear the combined breathing of the entire class.

"But who?" Stacy was the first mourner to show pain, to be dumbfounded by the event. "Who could do such a horrible thing to Miss Nichols?"

Nobody said a word. I suddenly heard the heavy thud of a newspaper on the floor. I looked around. There, in front of all the desks, lay the *Inquirer*. And guess who I saw, cowering like Public Enemy Number One?

Maybe it was an accident. Poor timing. But for the rest of the morning I didn't do much about anybody else's emotions because I had a lot of trouble controlling mine.

Lunch hour didn't make things much better. My co-workers managed to be solicitous at arm's length. Philly Prep doesn't have niceties like tenure, and with contract renewals coming up, maybe there was fear of consorting with a possible criminal. I was therefore as sought after as someone showing symptoms of the Black Death might be.

Caroline Finney dared direct contact. "Dear Amanda," she said as we waited for our lunches, "I know what you must be going through."

Caroline had taught Latin for thirty years. The last violent death she'd been aware of was Julius Caesar's. Still, her kindness was touching, but brief. She trundled off to a far table, and I sat down at my usual spot.

I poked at my lunch, murmuring acknowledgments to staff members as they passed by and listening to the muted whispers around me. I knew I was being discussed. Or perhaps I was becoming hopelessly paranoid. I tasted the corned beef hash and had little trouble renouncing it and the lunchroom.

The park across the street had a few picnicking students enjoying the first clear day in weeks. We ignored each other.

I stepped across a glittering puddle, admiring the impressionistic haze of trees filled with still-curled leaves. I found a vacant bench and sat there thinking and munching a hard roll I had saved from my lunch tray.

"Share your bench, lady?" Gus's voice was much more controlled than it had been this morning. "Or will the kids gossip about us?"

The kids speculated endlessly about single teachers' private lives, although they didn't really believe we had any. They had already linked me with Gus, with a gym teacher, with the sixty-year-old chemistry teacher, and probably with several others. A year ago, between a gone-to-seed Olympic skier and a chronically angry accountant, I had dated Gus once or twice. We found out that we were friends. Nothing more. But, more important, nothing less. I patted the bench for him to sit down.

"I wanted to apologize for this morning," he said. "I felt crazy. I also acted that way."

"It's understandable."

"Listen. I've been thinking. Did the cops check out phone calls? She probably called somebody from your house. Because, otherwise, how did the, uh, somebody, know she was there?"

How, indeed. Unless, of course, I'd told the somebody. A somebody so eager to see her about something troubling. Why was Gus so emphatically ignoring that bit of real-life history? I felt guilty even thinking that way. "Maybe she was followed from the bus," I said too brightly. Gus couldn't follow anybody with his bad leg. I wanted him to know I wasn't considering him a suspect. I wondered why it felt so important to pass on that message.

"What bus?"

"She said she'd gotten off one and come to my house."

"She was riding a bus at dawn?"

"I don't understand it, either."

The warning bell rang across the street, and we walked back. The kids, locked in a spring trance, didn't follow our exemplary behavior.

"The phone's more likely," Gus said, annoying me. "It was dark. It was raining. If somebody followed her, why didn't he, uh—I mean, if he was going to kill her, then why not do it in the street?"

"As awful as this sounds, Gus, I wish he had."

My last-period class was agitated. After all, it was their class she'd missed, probably because of being dead at the time.

I'd stopped encouraging discussion of Liza's death after the newspaper incident. But when we finished reviewing a snippet or two of *Macbeth*, I set the class to work writing sympathy notes to Mrs. Nichols. They became silent except for the sound of pencil chewing and the mournful, leaden sighs that in-class writing automatically produces.

A quarter of an hour before the end of class, the office monitor appeared with a note. Lance Zittsner was wanted in the office.

"He's absent," I told the monitor, who frowned, grimaced, shrugged at the class, and then checked his piece of paper. "Okay, then Michael Rizzio," he said.

The class stared at Michael and softly speculated.

When Michael reappeared, looking smug and self-important, he said that Carl Worman was wanted. He didn't even call Carl by his detested nickname, "The Vermin." I became anxious.

The Vermin reappeared with the same cockiness that Michael had shown. "They said to say they apologize for the interruptions."

"What's going on, Carl?"

"They said not to say."

"Who are they?"

"Oh, Miss Putnam and ... them."

I watched him write a hurried note and fling it across the aisle, where it was retrieved, read with exaggerated interest, and passed on. I declined to intercept it, since everyone who read it did some intense eyebrow jiggling in my direction.

The office monitor reappeared with another note. "Do you know how the ancients treated messengers of ill tidings?" I asked sweetly.

"Wha?"

"Never mind."

I read the note. Helga Putnam's perfect penmanship requested my appearance as soon as school was over.

* * *

Sitting rigidly behind her desk, her nose glowing like a signal beam, she greeted me. "Him," she said, tossing her tight curls to the right.

"Afternoon," he said. Under his corduroy jacket, Mackenzie wore a pale blue turtleneck, perfectly color coordinated with his eyes.

Helga lowered her voice and hissed in my direction. "I've told him everything."

C.K. dredged himself out of the chair. "We'll use Dr. H.'s office, okay, Helga?" he said.

She winced at the irreverent use of her name and her master's. I'd always thought of the two of them as Victor Frankenstein and Igor in drag. She rushed in before us and cleared the desk of his precious, jargon-laden papers, and then she left.

I sat down in front of the polished desk. "I feel like a kid with a detention."

His eyes were exceedingly blue, even if he hadn't been wearing that sweater. Blue enough to warrant some of his insufferable self-assurance.

He walked over to the long, high window facing the park. When he spoke, his voice was melancholy. "Miss Pepper, we have a new problem."

"Then I'll pass. The old one's enough for me, thanks."

"I stand corrected. We have the same problem with a new and puzzling factor. I'd like to go over yesterday's events one more tahm."

"Mackenzie, do you have a learning disability? Nothing's changed, you know. Just check your notebook. If you've got problems with note-taking skills, I can help. I teach that. Otherwise, I'll be going along. I have work to do."

"Miss Peppah, Miss Peppah." He turned to face me,

his long body silhouetted against the afternoon glare. "I do 'preciate your pedagogical responsibilities and rapier-lahk wit. However, I also have work to do. The big difference is that my work gets done first. Get it? So, go over it once again."

I controlled a real need to cry in frustration or punch him out and droned my way through the introduction. "...so I tried to call her, but nobody answered, so I went back to my class and—"

"Stop right there."

"Don't you want to know how I found the body? And how poor Mrs. Steinman took so long on her walker? You loved that part yesterday."

"Tastes change. It's the phone call today."

"Why?"

"Because Miss Helga says Liza was here with you yesterday."

I could feel that atavistic blush again. With Mackenzie around to put roses in my cheeks, I'd save a lot of cosmetics. "Oh, God."

"The Deity may understand you, Miss Peppah, but I most certainly do not."

"This is sort of embarrassing." I had the distinct feeling I'd used that line with him before.

"I trust I'm up to handlin' it."

I looked away and did a fast mumble. "I lied yesterday. To Helga. Well, not *really* a lie. I let her think what she wanted to. I never *said* that Liza was in the building. I just said I'd give her a message when I saw her. Which, I swear, I really hoped would be any minute."

"Ah," he said. He sucked in his bottom lip and ruminated. He seemed to think about as slowly as he spoke. "What you'd call a little white lie, is that it? Not a nasty, real lie, because you didn't say the words."

He leaned over me. The scent of his after-shave

stirred irrelevant emotions. "I hate games," he said without expression. Then he moved away, sat down in Havermeyer's chair, and put his feet up on the sacred desk. "Ah, you probably get that way bein' around kids all day," he said.

"Wait a minute! The kids—the kids you've been talking to—didn't they tell you Liza was absent?"

"Sure did. Anyway, I knew it before I got here."

So much for self-control. Maybe Mackenzie drummed up business by driving people to violence. I exhaled, and my breath was steaming. "You say you hate games? Then what do you call what you just did?" I stood up. "Good day, Officer," I said with all the outraged dignity I could muster.

"Sit down," he said, and I did. I even stayed quiet, which feat should have proved that I am not the kind to murder on impulse. "Liza couldn't be here for class because she died between one and two yesterday afternoon. During your lunch hour or right when class started. But she might have come to school before her class. You might have met up with her in your room."

"But I said—"

"You've said lots of things. And they're confusin'. You're a confusin' person. And a person who lives a few minutes away by car. You could have gone home without her or with her, become angry, pushed her against that fireplace, panicked, and left again. I understan' you usually spend that hour in the teachers' lounge, but not yesterday."

"Because I stopped smoking, and I didn't want to be around—"

"You could go home and be back here in time for class."

"You make me sound like a professional assassin!

Don't you need a motive?" I began to doubt my own innocence. I must be guilty to be treated this way.

He shrugged. "It'll appear. Eventually."

"Listen, talk to Gus Winston. I had lunch with him. And then I saw him when I went down to the office. I'm sure he'll remember."

"He has. So what? There were about forty minutes in between. Anyway, why'd you find it necessary to leave your class unattended and go to the office?"

"To call Liza. To remind her where she should be. I was understandably furious. She'd done this before."

He pulled his feet off the desk and leaned toward me. "Let's get this straight. You were angry with her, but at the same time you lied—white lie or what have you—to protect her?" He shook his head sadly. "Furthermore, it's mah impression you called Fargo, North Dakota, not your home."

"Helga Putnam is so worried we'll abuse the office—use up too many pencils or rubber bands or ditto masters, or make toll calls—that I said 'Fargo' just to hear her gasp. It was a joke."

"Or a sure-fahr way to make her remember where you were, then."

"Like an alibi?" I couldn't believe this. "Do you really think I killed Liza Nichols?"

He stood up to leave. He turned back to me when he reached the door, and he looked depressed. "I really think, Miss Peppah, that you ask too many questions and you don't give nearly enough answers."

Five

MACKENZIE LEFT ME ALONE. MAYBE HE hoped I'd take a cyanide tablet and lighten his caseload.

I listened to the end-of-day noises in the outer office. Someone ran the duplicating machine. Someone laughed and dropped a ring of jangling keys.

I spent seven minutes feeling sorry for myself, wishing I could retroactively cancel my decision to stop smoking. If my habit had only persisted one day longer, if I had only inhaled one user-friendly cigarette in the teachers' lounge on Monday, at alibi time, I wouldn't be on my way to the gallows. I never realized that not smoking could kill you, too.

But seven minutes of rewriting history is long enough. There were no more sociable noises coming from outside Havermeyer's stuffy office. Just the occasional taps of Helga Putnam's typewriter.

Luckily, my eleventh-grade class had completed *The Scarlet Letter* a few weeks earlier, and Hester Prynne was fresh on my mind. If she could walk the streets wearing her scarlet *A*, then I could face Igor out there.

Helga eyed me slyly, lowering one eyelid, pursing her lips with distaste for my dastardly deeds, but I held my head high and glided toward the telephone. How inspiring, how useful, the classics could be.

I wasn't going to wait in the suburbs while Mackenzie shuffled and bumbled around. He didn't seem too swift, and even with great detectives, there were cases that dragged on forever. This was going to be one of them if Mackenzie kept focusing on me. Meanwhile, I was getting back to my normal life. I dialed Beth's number.

"I'm staying home tonight," I told her. "I love you and appreciate all you want to do, but home's much easier and more convenient."

Beth made major use of words like "dangerous" and "foolish." But Beth had always considered anything urban to be blighted.

"Beth, thank you. I know you care, but if nothing else, I have to feed Macavity."

Back in my deserted classroom, I gathered up a textbook and the pile of sympathy notes I'd take to Liza's mother. I straightened the window shades, convincing myself I had not been the murderer's target. My house was no more than an unfortunate setting. I was therefore in no danger.

My room looked in order. I opened my pocketbook to get my car keys—one of my self-defense lessons was always to have keys ready before needed.

And then I saw it.

"Damn!" I'd forgotten the package, the bear, the five-hundred-dollar gift for "honey." Mackenzie would be thrilled anew to find me withholding evidence.

Liza's mother lived in an area that hadn't yet been declared chic and resold at ten times its original price. The row homes, three white steps up from the sidewalk, were not ornamented with window boxes and shutters in authentic colonial hues, as were those on my street. In-

stead, turquoise-and-white aluminum awnings hung
over front doors, and in a few instances, imitation stone
facing was inexplicably plastered over the original brick.

The street was crowded. In my neighborhood, people leave when they reproduce. Our tiny quarters are
too small to house several affluent middle-class generations. But here, where the houses were no larger, no
such philosophy reigned. I drove carefully, avoiding
balls, skates, hockey pucks, and small bodies. I found a
space near Mrs. Nichols's house and rang her doorbell,
a bouquet of early tulips and the packet of sympathy
notes in my free hand.

The woman who opened the door had an ample figure, but she looked deflated nonetheless.

"Is Mrs. Nichols in? I'm Amanda Pepper and I—"

"Come in, Amanda, come in. I've wanted so to meet
you." She made sociable gestures of welcome, leading
me toward a long brocaded sofa that filled one wall of the
small living room. "So pretty," she said of the flowers.
"Sit down, sit down. So nice to finally meet Liza's best
friend, and—" And then her voice liquefied and I could
feel recent events flood back into her consciousness. She
looked confused and fumbled for words, shook her
head, and hurried into another room with the flowers.

I looked down at my hands, embarrassed again by
the "best friend" label.

Mrs. Nichols returned, settling on a stiff, ornate chair
next to the television console. The furniture looked
plucked in toto from a late-night commercial. The
matching brocaded sofa and chairs were draped with
crocheted antimacassars, the marble-topped occasional
tables, covered with photographs, ashtrays, "conversation pieces," coasters, and lamp bases that were porcelain
ladies-in-waiting from one of the Louis's courts. Every
busy inch was shining, immaculate, and loved.

"I came to say how sorry I am. I brought notes from the class, her students. I wish I knew what else to say."

"Amanda," Mrs. Nichols said forcefully, "I know. I understand. I—I feel sorry for you, too." She sniffed and ran a puffy hand over her eyes. She was a small, plump woman, and hints of Liza's beauty were still evident inside her puffed features. "I know you had nothing to do with it." She shook her blue-gray hair. "I told them that." She pulled a crumpled tissue out of her dress pocket. "I told them."

"Who?"

"The police. Those detectives. A skinny black man and a big white one. They came last night, to—" her voice dwindled to a whisper—"to...tell me." She closed her eyes, then blew her nose. "The white one came this morning again. To ask me...things...about ...my baby!" She buried her head in her hands, the tissue pressed to her face.

I went over and crouched by her side, holding her arm until the sobbing stopped. When she spoke again, her voice quavered. "It doesn't make sense. Who would hurt my baby? Do you know? You were so close, the two of you."

I winced. "I don't know, Mrs. Nichols. I don't know."

"I was so happy when you two became friends, when she started staying with you. I always wanted the best for her. She stayed with good families, rich families, important people, when I worked for them. She lived in their houses, ate their food, wore the same clothing. You couldn't tell her apart from their children. She belonged there. She always belonged there."

My legs were cramping, and I stood up. Mrs. Nichols grabbed my hand. "You understand?" she demanded. "You understand?"

I nodded, although I didn't understand at all.

Her voice became dreamy. "I used to watch the children in the neighborhood, and I could tell, right from the beginning, that Liza didn't belong here. She was different, special. When she got so wild in high school, it broke my heart. And then, the acting, and wanting to go to New York, and—" she brushed something imaginary away with her hand—"and then, look, it all started happening the right way. Like magic. Like I always dreamed. Engaged to Hayden Cole and..."

Mrs. Nichols was deep, deep inside that old dream of hers. She smiled proudly, and I knew she had momentarily forgotten again. And then she looked around the crowded room as if something had leaped out of a corner, and her face collapsed. She stood up and leaned against the television console. Its top was covered with framed pictures of Liza. Some were ads cut from slick magazines. Some were fuzzy snapshots of a young Liza. Mrs. Nichols touched the silver frame of her daughter's engagement portrait. "She was beautiful," she whispered.

"Yes," I agreed.

She walked over to the sofa, near me. "The police, they asked if anything was bothering her. Why?"

"I think it's just something they ask in these situations."

"How could she be troubled? She was marrying Hayden Cole! She was going to be a senator's wife, maybe something even more someday. She was going to live in a mansion. Is that something to bother a girl? Since the day she was born, since her father ran out on us, I've worked every day to get back her real place in life. I gave her speech lessons, dance lessons. I never let her feel she was a little girl whose daddy ran away with a cheap—who didn't care if we had a cent or a way to live like decent people. It was all for her. For Liza."

I understood why Liza didn't find it easy to talk to her mother. The woman had decided how the world worked a long time ago, and how to make it work for her, and she wouldn't have been interested in any of her daughter's opposing theories. She cataloged half a dozen more special lessons given her daughter. Modeling, singing, on and on. It reminded me of geisha training.

"Of course, she was high-strung," Mrs. Nichols said. "Especially lately. But all brides get cold feet. If she'd had any important worries, I would have known. We were very close. You must know that."

I had a sudden painful realization of how far apart we all stand from one another, how single-minded we all must be in what we want and what we choose to see.

"Mrs. Nichols, you must be exhausted." And if she wasn't, I was. "You should be resting. I just wanted to express my sympathy. Is there anything I can do to help you through this?"

"You aren't leaving?" She looked terrified. "Let me fix you something. Coffee, tea, please?"

So I followed her into the tiny kitchen that was really a side slice of the dining room. It was decorated with the same heavy hand as the living room. The toaster was covered by a gingham rooster with a skirt. The salt-and-pepper shakers were a ceramic angel and devil. Magnets shaped like bananas and pears held a calendar and notes to the refrigerator.

Mrs. Nichols busied herself with the kettle. "It's so awful. Things go on like normal, as if nothing had happened. The mail comes, a check for a job she did. A phone call. Her answering service. I don't know what to

do with it, I feel bad throwing it away, just like that...."
She turned on the water tap and filled the kettle.

There was a small pile of mail on the table, all addressed to Liza, all opened. I had a good theory as to why Liza had her personal mail, or packages, sent to school, not home.

The calendar on the refrigerator was a sad witness to change. The future was all arranged in its small white squares. Tonight, Tuesday, had a notation: Dinner—H —7:00 P.M. Friday, Saturday, and Sunday all had "PPH"—Philadelphia Playhouse, I assumed, inked across the bottom of the squares. There were more notes and notices for Liza behind magnetic grapes and plums, chickens and cows: "Special rehearsal, Saturday A.M.," a list, ripped from a magazine, of "good, moderately priced wines," and, farthest from the calendar, a longer missive signed "Mom."

"Liza," it said, "I'll be back around 6. Ans. Serv. called—call agency, maybe job Wed.? Also Winnie— call back."

Winnie? As in a little gold bear? Somebody called Winnie, not "honey"?

"I know I have to throw things away," Mrs. Nichols said, "but I can't. It feels too . . ."

I put cups and placemats on the dining room table. "Mrs. Nichols, who is Winnie?"

She shrugged and seated herself. "A friend. She had so many. I never met most of them. Models, teachers, the Coles' friends. Why?" But she didn't really require an answer.

We sat in a tiny dining room heavy with furniture scaled for another setting. The whole house felt squeezed, condensed, as if Mrs. Nichols had stocked up for bigger, better days.

Mrs. Nichols reminisced about the past, her face softening as she spoke about the young Liza.

A clock in the living room went through an elaborate chiming tune, and Mrs. Nichols glanced at her watch. "Oh, my," she said, "I didn't realize how long I was talking. I'll just tidy these," she said, gathering up our cups. "Mr. Winston will be here soon."

"Gus?"

Mrs. Nichols nodded.

It was as natural for Gus to pay a condolence call as it was for me. More so. He had dated Liza, and he had worked and acted with her.

Winnie? Nobody had ever called Gus Winston that in my hearing. But it would be like Liza to rename him on her own and think it was cute. Still. A five-hundred-dollar trinket? A love gift?

What was there left between them?

How could I know so many people without knowing anything about them?

It was dark when I pulled into my parking lot. I walked onto a nearly deserted Walnut Street. A woman shuffled along in a coat over a nightgown. She wore fisherman's wading boots and carried a bottle in a brown paper bag. A man with a briefcase walked double-time.

I turned the corner toward my street and became truly alone.

Imitation colonial gaslights stand at each end of my authentically colonial street. They throw an antiquated haze over the corners, leaving even nearby cobblestones and hitching posts shadowy suggestions and the middle of the block a dark haze.

I flinched when a breeze knocked a loose shutter, when a spray of pussy willow in a nearby tub swayed.

"Stop it!" a muffled voice cried, and I gasped, until I realized it was only the angry sound of a woman inside one of the houses. Still, the voice triggered echoes in my memory, Liza crying out the same words.

The small of my back tensed. Clutching my house keys, I reassured myself that I was alone and safe, and I turned around to confirm it.

There was nothing near the puddle of light at the corner. Nothing behind me. I turned back.

And saw a shadow shrink and pull into itself.

You're making it up, Amanda. Hallucinating. There's nothing but stairways and planters.

The moon moved farther into a cloud bank, and the street became darker, heavier with fluid shadow.

There's nothing there.

Still, I was afraid to run, afraid to make noise, afraid to alert the nothingness to my fear. I tiptoed silently, clutching my keyring like a talisman.

But something was somewhere.

I could feel it. Could sense it, as if its body heat sent out rays.

I tried not to breathe, listening, waiting for a sound, a lunge.

And then I bolted for my doorway and jammed in the key, barely able to see through a sudden blur of tears. I looked one last time to the right and saw, this time for sure, a tiny arc of light as a cigarette fell to the ground. Then I saw the shadow again change, enlarge, and pull away from the wall.

I didn't wait to see the form take definite shape.

I threw open the door of my house and ran in, screaming at the top of my lungs.

Six

I PRESSED MY BACK AGAINST THE INSIDE OF the front door, trapped. Rational or not, I was afraid to move and call for help, as if only my body weight kept my house safe.

Who was he?

I strained to hear a move outside, footsteps, anything.

What was he doing?

But all I could hear was my own pulse, beating heavily in my eardrums.

What was he waiting for?

You imagined it, I told myself. You've been under a strain. I listened again.

What did he want?

The room pulsed, as if the whole house were having an anxiety attack along with me, breathing irregularly, hearing gradations in the silence.

I pried myself off the door and went toward the phone. The back of my little house seemed to recede, like the horizon in a nightmare, the phone shimmering farther and farther back.

En route, I passed the radio on the kitchen counter. Always leave the radio on, so your house will sound inhabited, I heard from some brain-scrapbook of helpful hints. One or two synapses over, a corollary message flashed—"Do it when you *leave* the house, dummy," but I wasn't in the mood to quibble. With one hand, I turned on the radio; with the other, I lifted the telephone receiver. Loud wailing metal filled the room; I couldn't as easily hear my heart beating away my life. I listened hungrily. It felt so normal, so ordinary, to be standing in the kitchen tuned in to my ex-D.J.'s station.

As if nothing had happened.

And it probably hadn't. Or if it had, he'd gone away by now. He had probably not been there in the first place, and certainly not waiting for me. I was being a fool. Mackenzie would have a heyday, making fun of me. I hung up the phone.

And then the doorbell rang.

I willed myself invisible. I was numb and lightheaded.

I was also incredibly stupid. The person outside knew I was in here. Had watched me enter.

The bell rang again.

"Go away!" I screamed, finally out of my paralysis. "I've got a gun! Joe, get the gun! We've called the police!" I added for good measure, horrified that I hadn't. I picked up the receiver again.

"Now," I instructed myself. "Dial." My throat hurt from wanting to cry and from the shouting. My hand trembled. "Now," I repeated. I was holding the phone, but at the same time opening kitchen drawers in search of a weapon, scanning the house for a suddenly invented secret exit, a hidden passage. "Dial."

Call the police.

And know that they won't get here in time.

"The police are coming!" I screamed above the radio's beat.

"Police!" the voice outside echoed. It didn't make sense. I put back the receiver, turned off the radio, and tiptoed to the door.

"—kenzie," I heard. "Please open up."

Kenzie? Mackenzie? The one who hated games? Mackenzie had been lurking, following me? Terrifying me for sport?

This was a citizen's case. The Philadelphia Police Department could add this one to their list of woes. My hands shook as I unbolted and unchained the door.

He smiled down on me.

"You *bastard!*" I was too angry to speak coherently, and my voice was high and strident, my words a pile of anger, tumbling out. "How *dare* you? How could you? What kind of sadistic—you should be thrown off the force! Arrested!"

He closed the door behind him and watched me, his eyebrows raised.

"I won't stand for any of this anymore! I'm not a criminal. Even if I were—even if you think I am—we have rights, dammit. What kind of monster wouldn't say something? Identify himself?"

"I tried," he said. "Several times."

"You did not!"

"Perhaps I spoke too softly, but mos' people get upset if their neighbors know the police are visitin' them. Again."

"A word! One single word! Somebody was murdered here yesterday—how do you think that makes me feel when a lunatic policeman plays games and—"

My anger dissipated abruptly, along with my fear, and I had nothing left to hold me up. I sagged onto the sofa and began to cry, hating myself for it, but unable to stop.

"Miss Peppah, I—don't go cryin', now! I mean I didn't expect a royal welcome, but this is somewhat much, don't you think?" He casually straddled one of the ladder-back chairs and regarded me.

I wiped my eyes and looked at him. The skin was pulled tight across his cheekbones. There were shadows like bruises under his light eyes.

He shifted on the chair. "Did somethin' happen? Somethin' hurt you? Is this some kind of game? Or do you want me to play detective, to guess the meanin' of all this?"

I didn't say anything. I had half expected some Southern gentlemanly response on his part. Which I would have rejected. Heatedly. Instead, he yawned and looked around the room. I snuffled and wiped my eyes, afraid my mascara had run and furious that I could have such trivial, recidivist concerns at such a time.

"Miss Peppah," he said, "conversation appears to be difficult this evening. Frankly, I don't know what's goin' on. I know I was harsh this afternoon. But surely you understand, and aren't you carryin' a grudge too far?"

What were we talking about? I had only carried my grudge from the front doorstep into my living room.

He shook his head, stood up, and walked to the door. "I'm too tired for this. I'm parked in front, blockin' your street, so I can't stay anyway. Listen, I tried to call you at your sister's, and she told me you were back. I was on my way home anyway, so I dropped by to tell you in person. Somehow, I thought it was a kind, considerate gesture."

"Parked outside?" I said. There hadn't been any car at all.

Mackenzie exhaled loudly. "You gonna give me a ticket?" He muttered something to himself. "Listen, forget I was ever here. I'll call tomorrow."

"Wait, please," I said. "You had something to tell me?"

"Didn't think you heard. Yes, I did. I do. Here goes: You are no longer in any way under suspicion, Miss Pepper. Now, good night."

"Don't go." I felt like a fool, too much of one even to explain myself to the man. "I'll make coffee. Or wine. Wine's better. Please stay and explain. I'll be all right." I felt like a preschooler swearing I'd behave if I could stay up a little longer. I busied myself finding glasses, wine, and my bearings and avoiding Mackenzie's face.

Meanwhile, Mackenzie stayed silent.

After due deliberation, I left the jug of white wine in the refrigerator and took out the good bottle of red that Mackenzie had included in his analysis of me. Facing his sarcasm was how I belatedly chose to demonstrate bravery. "Well?" I asked. "Who did it?"

"Beats me. I only know you didn't."

"You found a clue, then?"

"In a manner of speakin'."

I set my two good wineglasses on the table, poured the house best, and settled across from him. "To celebrate my innocence," I said, lifting my glass. "Well, what kind of clue did you find? A fingerprint?"

He shook his head. "'Fraid not," he said. "Nothing clear, anyway. It was rainy and chilly Monday. Liza's visitor probably wore gloves. We found something better than fingerprints. We found a witness."

"Somebody saw it happen?" I felt dizzy with relief. A witness. The bad guys would be identified and locked up, and I wouldn't hallucinate and see demons in doorways anymore.

He shook his head. "Not a witness to the crahm. A witness who established that you were in school all day long."

I shrugged.

"You're not impressed?"

"I knew where I was all along."

"You don't want to know who?"

I shrugged again. "A teacher walking by?"

He shook his head. "It was Lance Zittsner."

"Lance? Lancelot Zittsner cleared me?" It figured. My maiden effort at being a damsel in distress brought me a belching, gangling Lancelot. "But he was absent today. How did you find him? Or how did he find you?"

"He came to school for homeroom and came back for his bus pass after school. The kid cuts a lot. Actually, 'bout half your school cuts a lot. But Lance was there yesterday at lunchtime, and he says he saw you dozin' at your desk."

Mackenzie stood up. "I'll try to recreate the scene, impress you with my detectin'." He shuffled around, scratched his stomach, stared at the ceiling, and somehow wrapped a little Zittsner essence around him. "See, like they sometimes don't lock their rooms," he said, his voice a funny Southern imitation of a brassy Philadelphia accent. "Miss Pepper, she forgets maybe half the time. And she keeps our work folders in a file cabinet, you know? So reports are coming out, and like I get a car if I pass everything."

Mackenzie dropped the Lance-talk and posture. He grinned at me. "You see?"

"Not quite."

"Clue. He wasn't going to change his grades or take anything. Think."

"That doesn't leave much except bringing things in. Like papers to put in his folder, I bet. Then he'd claim I never graded them. How on earth did you get him to confess?"

Mackenzie sat back down. "The bamboo splinters under the nails. Always works. That, and some other esoteric, brilliant, and secret stuff."

I spent a moment wondering how often Lance or other students had pulled that scam on me, and then I shelved that problem for another, easier time. "Mackenzie," I said, "did you ever really suspect me?"

"Of what? Murder? Or insanity? You aren't totally explainable, you know. The sweeping, the North Dakota call—even the way you answered the door just now...."

A siren screamed in the distance. Mackenzie glanced sideways at the sound. "My car—" he began, but he didn't sound overly concerned. I poured more wine.

"About the way I answered the door—" I felt my color rise until I was sure my cheeks matched my hair. "I'm sorry. It wasn't about you. I thought it was, of course. But I see that it wasn't."

He leaned across the table. "Are you under the impression that you're making sense right now?"

I cleared my throat. "When I came home, a few minutes before you knocked, there was somebody else on this street. Somebody waiting, hiding. He started out, and I screamed and ran inside. Anyway, then you arrived and I thought you'd been the one lurking there, playing some macho game."

"You sure about this?" Mackenzie looked actively interested for a change.

I nodded. "There was even a light, a cigarette or match, something, dropped to the ground."

He looked as though deep inside he'd coiled, gotten ready to pounce. He was still slouching on the outside, but the immediate tension in him was contagious.

"It was probably nothing. A coincidence," I said. "Someone on his way home. I mean, why would anyone be hiding, waiting for me?"

Now that is what I would have said if I'd been facing me, scared, across a table. I waited for him to play Big Daddy and reassure me everything was my silly imagination and that I shouldn't worry. But he remained silent, those waves of concentrated energy bouncing off him.

"Maybe you should stay at your sister's a while longer," he finally said.

"C'mon," I prompted him. "It was *nothing*. I'm not completely rational. I've been under a strain. I'm being a foolish, hysterical *female*."

He stared at me. "I hadn't thought of it that way," he said.

It was a relief when we were interrupted by the telephone. But only for a moment. And then I had to cope with my mother. She claimed to be beside herself, and she really was upset, I could tell. She'd forgotten to use her discount system, and there was no whine or echo.

I tried to soothe her. Long-distance anxiety is about as useless an emotion as I can think of. "It's all right now," I said. "Everything's over. I'm fine."

I apologized for not allowing her to worry sooner, for leaving it up to Beth to pass on the bad news. And then, once she was reassured that I was alive, she stopped worrying about my fears and resumed her life-long monologue. She told me how often she'd told me things. How often she'd warned me about urban crime, about being headstrong and willful, living alone in a hotbed of depravity, of how sick all this was making her.

I was impressed by the elasticity of her basic, all-purpose lecture. It had never before needed to stretch to include my finding a dead colleague in my living room, but she gave it a tug and a poke, and it made do.

"Mom?" I interrupted a detailed discourse on what this was doing to my father, "I can't talk now." I pulled out the only ammunition strong enough to intercept my mother's barrage of worries and guilt. "I have a date here," I said loudly and clearly.

My mother's tirade ended as sharply as if she'd whacked off the rest with a machete.

Within a few moments, I was able to hang up. "I'm sorry I used you that way," I told the detective. "She wouldn't have ever stopped, otherwise."

For some reason, he looked like a farm boy in city clothes. "I don't feel used," he said, "and I'm not sorry at all." He looked directly at me, his eyes blue and interested. The farm boy disappeared. So did the cop.

"Are you suggesting something in your own oblique way?" I asked, meeting his look headlong.

He shrugged and raised one eyebrow.

"And what might it be?"

"You're a bright, imaginative woman. The possibilities are endless. Think about it."

"You're somewhat smug, Mackenzie."

He smiled confidently, proving my point.

I yawned.

"You've got a unique style yourself," he said.

"Sorry. That wasn't deliberate. This has been one of the longest days of my life, and then the wine...This morning at Beth's seems years away." And then, finally,

I remembered all the way back to the start of the day. "Officer Mackenzie," I began nervously.

"Officer Mackenzie? What would your mother think of your callin' your date that? Call me C.K."

"It's not easy to call anybody C.K. What does it stand for?"

"Is that what's botherin' you?"

"No. It's—I forgot to tell you something this afternoon."

He tensed, as if bracing for a disappointment.

"I picked up something yesterday while I was taking things out of the mailboxes. To cover for Liza's absence, remember?" I reminded myself that I was no longer a suspect. I was an honorable, if forgetful, citizen. I wished he wouldn't look at me that way.

He nodded, encouraging me to continue.

"There was a package in Liza's mailbox. I meant to give it to you today, but you were so—I forgot, that's all. I forgot it yesterday, too. But my niece opened it this morning, and I think it might be important." I retrieved the box and its wrapping paper.

"Interesting," he said, holding the bear by its chain. "But why important?"

I showed him the sales slip. Both his eyebrows rose at the price tag for the charm. "Liza bought it," I said. "She had it delivered to school, not home. Her mother opens her mail."

"A surprise for Mama?"

"Not likely, is it?"

"A bear." He sipped his wine.

"Winnie the Pooh," I answered. "A copy of the Ernest Shepherd illustrations."

"You study that kind of thing to be an English teacher?"

"To be an aunt in good standing."

"It's a heavy chain," he said. "Long, too. Masculine —if you're a gold-chain kind of man, that is. For the fiancé, Cole, you think?"

I did not think, and neither did he, judging by his expression.

"Guess we can check out Cole's birth date," he said, carefully putting the bear back into its plush box. "Who all did she call 'honey'?"

"Well, I'm not sure it's that. I saw a message at Mrs. Nichols's house today. For Liza, from Winnie. That makes better sense for that particular bear. But Mrs. Nichols didn't know who Winnie was."

"Don't you?"

"Me?" His eyes reminded me of lakes in Maine. Tempting, but ice cold. "Listen, Augustus Winston is not the kind to—"

"Ah," C. K. Mackenzie said, "who is?" He looked at the closed jeweler's box. "I've gone through lists of her friends, the school people, the modeling agency, the Playhouse." He flipped through his ratty brown notebook. "Nope. Not a possible Winnie in the group. Except for Augustus Winston III."

His eyes lost some of their iciness. "But how would he have known she was at your house? That secretary would have mentioned any personal calls made to the school, wouldn't she?"

I didn't know what my role as a good citizen now was. I didn't know what a sane but humane human being with a desire to have a murderer caught should do next. Finally, it boiled down to two factors: I didn't want to create trouble for Gus, but even more than that, I didn't want to find any more corpses because I had withheld a piece of information. "I told him," I said, but softly, "at lunch yesterday."

Mackenzie's eyes definitely thawed. "It may mean

nothing," he said. "Half the city knew she was here. She made three toll calls Monday morning."

I felt an automatic flare of annoyance—she hadn't asked permission. And then, ashamed, I quelled it.

"She called the Coles' house, the Bellingers' house, and a community hall where Cole was speaking. And God knows how many others who wouldn't register as tolls."

He stood up and raked his fingers through his hair. "Of course, nobody connected or got a coherent message, they say. Housekeeper and Hayden's manager took the calls. The Coles and Bellingers have extended service that doesn't charge for calls into the city, or record them. So I don't know if her calls were returned. I don't know whether she made other calls. I wish we still had snoopy old-time operators."

He flopped back onto the chair. "I was just at the Playhouse. Your friend Winston wasn't. Called to say he'd be late, I was told."

"There's nothing suspicious about that. He made a condolence call to Mrs. Nichols."

Mackenzie didn't seem interested. He pulled a rumpled playbill out of his pocket, smoothing its creases absently as he lay it on the table. It was a doubled-over mimeographed sheet. "They already made the cast changes for this weekend." He pointed to the third listing from the top. "Abbie will now be played by one Sarah Halvorsen."

I fingered the cheap paper. "They don't splurge on programs, do they?"

"Well, you know it's not much of a theater. Every one of them managed to tell me how he could and should have been in New York or Hollywood, what missed breaks he'd suffered."

He was interrupted by the blast of a car horn. He

looked annoyed; then he looked embarrassed. "My car! It's blocking the way. I forgot all about it."

Nice. With gold trinkets, unsolved murders, and a few glasses of wine I had charmed the cop into forgetfulness. I was a veritable Scheherazade. But I didn't have time to gloat, because Mackenzie was up and moving toward the door.

Damn the driver outside. He wasn't supposed to use my adorable street anyway. He deserved to be blocked.

Something whirled across the screen of my thoughts like a moth. "Wait!" I said, trying to catch it. "There's something. I—" There was another volley of honks from outside, and the moth-thought disintegrated.

"Yes?" Mackenzie said.

I shook my head. "It's gone again."

The horn blasted once, then three times in rapid succession. "Listen," he said, "if you remember, or hear anything strange, or are frightened by anyone again, give me a call." He jotted numbers on the back of the playbill and handed it to me. "Meanwhile, get some sleep. Lock up."

I could hear him soothe the other driver while I slipped locks and chains and double-checked them. Mackenzie had caused an atmospheric change that left with him. The house felt overly quiet and ominous again.

Still, I could call him if anything happened. I held the paper carefully and put it on the table, pouring another glass of wine. The cars drove away, and the street became silent. I read the playbill the same way I read cereal boxes and newspaper fillers, because they're there.

Desire Under the Elms. Ephraim Cabot played by Tony deBanco. Peter Cabot by Kevin Kelley. Simeon Cabot by Herman Schwartz. Abbie by Sarah Halvorsen.

It was a United Nations of a cast. The rest of the surnames were not as interesting. Harper, Beekman, Bayer, and Foster sounded like a second-rate advertising agency. Perhaps that's why they'd been given minor roles. I put the playbill aside and finished my wine. And then I just about finished the bottle, administering the liquid like a patient anesthesiologist. When I was numb enough, I washed up and went to bed, but not before I'd memorized the phone numbers Mackenzie had given me. Even so, I kept them and the telephone on the bed next to me. Eventually, Macavity, finally sure the shouting and shenanigans were over, snuggled in with me, sleeping on top of the playbill.

Seven

"LIKE I KNOW YOU DIDN'T DO ANYTHING bad, Miss Pepper, but still, I saved your neck, kind of. So I thought maybe..."

I watched Lance Zittsner hem and haw as he attempted academic blackmail. He perspired profusely and chewed his bottom lip, punishing it for not furnishing him with winning words.

"I mean, like my father always says, you scratch my back, I scratch yours," he said.

There was not a single inch of Zittsner I would consider scratching.

"You think I could like, pass?" he finally gasped.

I considered. If I failed him, I'd view that face, hear its symphonic belches, for another full year. "Tell me," I said, "do you still have the papers you wanted to put in my file?"

"The cop told you about them?" he asked.

I nodded. "However, if you have finally done the work, I'll accept it and grade it as late. For expediency's sake." I knew he hadn't a clue as to what "expediency" meant, but he'd consider it part of an abstruse pedagogical code.

"I'll get them," he said, hurrying out.

I was not suffused with guilt for abandoning academic ethics. Lance was heir apparent to the largest scrap metal business in Philadelphia. Would it help him to belch through *Macbeth* again next year? Would dangling participles or misplaced modifiers do much damage in a junkyard?

My first class straggled in, looking bored in advance. Word was out that the fun was over. Teacher wasn't being dragged away in leg irons. I tidied my desk, throwing away the plastic cup and refolding the newspaper. Liza's death had been moved off the front page by an impending transit strike. But I'd found a picture of Hayden Cole on page two, under the headline "Cole Vows War on Crime."

Hayden Cole, Republican candidate for State Senate, today pledged to fight the wave of urban crime in this state. Cole refused to comment on the violent death of his fiancée, actress Liza Nichols. Instead, he asked to be thought of as "only one of many victims of a plague of senseless violence, which I pledge to make my highest priority."

I rammed the paper into my pocketbook, trying to believe that Hayden Cole was not using Liza's death as fodder for another clichéd political speech. I told myself that he was keeping private feelings private.

I didn't believe me.

Gus didn't even try to think the best of the candidate. I was on my way to lunch when he walked up, started to say something, and then stopped. His eyes were on the newspaper jutting out of my bag, and his face grew dark and contemptuous.

"Did you see it?" he demanded. "Did you see how the unfeeling son of a bitch handled her—handled what's happened?" He limped down the stairs beside me, his knuckles white as he gripped the banister.

"Oh, Gus, in all fairness, what could he say? It must be awful to have newspaper people around all the time."

"Son of an ice-cold bitch. Making political hay of her death!" He clamped his mouth shut, but still looked like an explosion waiting to happen.

"How about skipping the lunchroom? How about we grab something in the park?" He halfheartedly shrugged at my suggestion and turned around like a sullen automaton. "Let me drop off my roll book," I said.

Helga Putnam greeted us with a nod of her tight curls. The day was warm, but she pulled her mud-colored cardigan around her shoulders and shuddered as we walked in. "There's a notice for you," she said. "And for him," she added to no one in particular.

There was no longer a name under Liza's mailbox. Helga was nothing if not efficient. The blank spot spoke volumes, with brass corners for punctuation. I read my notice:

> Memorial services for Liza Nichols will take place this Friday noon at Hill's Funeral Home, 15th and Hickory. Burial will follow the service at Mount Peace Cemetery. Any member of the staff wishing to attend must notify H. Putnam so that substitutes may be obtained. All students who attend are to be given excused absences for the day.
>
> There will also be a viewing Thursday evening from 6:00 P.M. on at the funeral home.

Gus and I walked silently across the street into the square. Lost in our own thoughts, we bought hot soft pretzels from a vendor and slathered them with mustard. But neither of us ate. We sat on a bench staring at the pretzels as if they were interesting but inedible artifacts.

"Oh, God, Mandy, I feel...I can't..." Gus's sigh was loud and jagged. "I can't come up for air. I mean, what was Liza to me? We had nothing left. She killed it, all of it. Why is it getting to me this way?"

He looked up at the sky and shuddered. "If you had asked me before—before this happened—I would have said I hated her. So why should I feel so..."

I reached over and touched his hand. It didn't relax around the misshapen pretzel.

"She was everywhere I was. At school, at the Playhouse. It drove me crazy when she was always there. But now, now it's worse. I can't get past her."

"It'll come, Gus. Eventually." I didn't know what to say, and I grabbed for the nearest bromide, hoping that it was true and that it would help.

"Even at the theater," he said. "My place. My real place. I know the old show-must-go-on routine, but I don't know why it should be so. We started rehearsals with a new Abbie last night, and it was so hard." He considered a moment. "Hard as in difficult, and hard as in unfeeling. Ghoulish. As if we were just replacing a rusted or ruined part of a machine."

I had no answers. I didn't even have real questions, so I tried to veer us onto a less emotional tack. "I saw the revised playbill," I said. "Mackenzie showed it to me."

Gus frowned when I mentioned the detective's name, but I ignored his expression.

"He came to my house last night bearing glad tidings. Listen, Gus." I must admit I embellished the tale of my rescue at the grubby hands of Sir Lancelot Zittsner. I invented a few extra curlicues and flourishes, and whatever I lost in hard truth, I gained by seeing the lines on Gus's face slowly dissolve into something like a smile.

I kept talking, while taking his emotional pulse. I didn't want to have fine print in our relationship.

"You know," I said, when we were well out of the high-tension area, "I understand what you meant when you said reminders of Liza are all around. I keep thinking about her, too. Every time I see Helga, I think of her as the office witch. And Dr. H—Liza called him Hemmenhawer. Even me. She called me—" I juggled possibilities while I cleared my throat, tried to look embarrassed about the nickname I frantically searched for. "She once watched a particularly bad class when I couldn't find a clear way to explain, oh, the difference between the objective correlative and a symbol."

"Christ, who could? Particularly with our kids."

"Sure, but I was going to try, right? Anyway, after that agonized little session, Liza called me 'Meander Pepper.'" I was very proud of that improvisation, and I took a moment to savor it before continuing. "I miss her silly tags for everything. Did she—did she have any special name for you, Gus?"

I couldn't decide whether that had been an example of a subtle segue or of steamrollering.

"Names? Several. Basically unacceptable in polite society. The least offensive one I can remember was 'Disgustus.'"

I watched him eat his pretzel and then light a cigarette. I hoped he wasn't as good a liar as I was.

We sat in silence. The trees were still bare, the patches of grass new and tentative, separated by hard, brown streaks, the scars of winter frosts. But the air was soft and promising, and its message had reached every housewife and nanny who'd spent the winter locked indoors with a child. They filled the park, sitting in clusters on benches, keeping an eye on nearby charges.

The children dug in the grassless spaces, ran and rode tricycles on the paths. I mentally changed places with the clusters of mothers, wondering how it would be to have very short, very cute people in one's caretaking, instead of Lance Zittsner *et cie*.

Of course, Lance himself was once presumably short and cute, so I realized I had more thinking to do on this subject.

The school bell across the street buzzed me angrily back to current choices. When we reached the double doors of the school, Gus turned to me. "I'm sorry if I seem distracted. The play's giving me a lot of trouble since . . . Anyway, would you consider doing me a favor and playing critic? We're rehearsing again tonight, and I'm really bothered by Halvorsen's performance, but I don't know if I'm being too harsh. You know the play. Can I bribe you with the addition of dinner at a new, good, cheap Italian place I found?"

"Augustus, I accept. I'd love it."

The Playhouse was a state of mind in a church school's auditorium. I had been there for performances, but this was my first rehearsal observance. I sat near the back and watched in the dubious comfort of an ancient cracked leather seat. The enthusiasm of the players, however, impressed me. They'd been performing *Desire Under the Elms* for several weekends now, but they treated the rehearsal as a new project. There was a slight edge of hysteria in their energy as they almost visibly prodded the pallid Sarah.

Sarah's yellow-white hair was pulled back into a knot, and her body, hard and muscular, would necessitate refittings of Liza's costumes. Nothing about her was reminiscent of her predecessor. Gus said that also applied to her acting ability.

Over wine and pasta, he'd shaken his head. "She's flat—not only physically, but emotionally. Sometimes it works for her. She's done some wonderful Noël Coward, for example. She can carry that off perfectly, understating, being dry. But I don't know about O'Neill. Trouble is, the woman who might have done better took a dinner theater job in Bucks County. So we're stuck."

"You're seeing her in contrast," I'd reminded him. "The audience won't. I won't."

So I sat in the dark theater, trying to study Sarah objectively.

Onstage, the rehearsal stopped for the third confrontation in as many minutes.

"I'll do it my own damned way!" Sarah shouted. "Let me at least try it!"

She'd make it. Little Sarah had a profound temper, and with some luck and guidance, she'd call on that passion to give substance to her part.

"He mumbles!" Sarah screamed a few minutes later. "No wonder I keep missing my goddamned cues!"

"Okay, Sarah, okay," Gus said from the first row. "Speak up, Eddie, would you?"

A young dark-haired man started to protest. Then he made a motion of disgust. "Right," he said, or I think he did, because now he was truly inaudible. But when he got back into his role, he managed to keep his voice strong, and Sarah seemed momentarily satisfied.

"Well, what a surprise. What brings you here? Now of all times? Morbid interest, is that it? Or are you auditioning?"

I didn't have to look over at the woman slithering between the rows of seats to recognize her blather.

Sissie Bellinger perched near me, fishing through her handbag.

"Gus invited me," I whispered.

Sissie nodded several times, as if she'd reached an important decision. She found a cigarette and lit it, flicking the ashes between the seats. "Actually," she said between drags, "I don't know why I'm here. Except that I love it. And I like keeping an eye on my investments."

She must have had eyes all over the place, because she hadn't bought her silk blouse, heavy gold earrings, or wafer-thin watch on the dividends of this company. "Halvorsen shouldn't have that role," Sissie said in what she probably considered a soft voice. "Pity. I could do it better. I acted once, did you know that? Have the police found out about it yet?"

"About your acting?"

"About Liza," Sissie snapped.

I shook my head. "I don't think so."

"They don't know what they're doing. That sluggish detective keeps coming back. Why, I don't know. And to the Coles'. Black man comes along with him. Because she phoned me! To make such a fuss over a call the housekeeper took! And meanwhile, a maniac is loose." She stubbed out her cigarette on the threadworn carpeting and lit another. "Unless, of course, he does know something," she added. "You think it's possible?"

"Mackenzie?"

"Whoever. Does he?"

"I don't—"

"Did Liza tell you something? That morning? Anything? When she came in?" Sissie's perfume was flowery but tart. "Did she tell you who—what made her so upset? Not that you should trust a word she'd say."

I was almost positive that Sissie had asked me the same questions with the same urgency two nights ago. But I couldn't be sure. I could only be certain that she had annoyed me in precisely the same way she was now doing.

"I can't hear myself!" Sarah screamed from the stage. "Somebody's carrying on in the auditorium!"

I slumped down in my seat, even though I hadn't been the one who'd offended Halvorsen's eardrums.

Sissie, however, gestured with contempt, scattering ashes on the seat in front of her. "Delusions of grandeur, every one of them. Liza, too. Be a star in New York. Be a Cole. Always trying on parts, thinking she could play anything. If everybody would be what they are, then—"

"I quit!" Sarah screamed. "I don't have to take this! I can't think straight."

Sissie looked toward the stage with no expression, then, without another word, stood up and slithered aisleward, and from there into the void beyond the theater.

"Okay," Gus said up front. "Let's call it a night. We're all tired, anyway."

The cast walked off the stage. Sarah made her descent slowly, glaring into the dark auditorium as she moved.

"One minute," Gus said. "In case anybody hasn't heard, Liza's funeral is Friday noon at Hill's. There's a viewing tomorrow night from six o'clock on. We'll start rehearsal late tomorrow, around eight-thirty." His voice was firm and resolute, as if he'd practiced his little speech.

I walked toward the cluster of actors. "I wasn't the

one making noise," I said defensively. Sarah sniffed in my direction and stalked away.

"We all recognized the voice," Gus said. He lowered his voice. "If there were some way to take her money and ban her from entering the building, we'd do it." He turned to the group of players. "Everybody, this is Amanda Pepper. She was not the noisemaker. I'll be with you in a minute, Mandy."

Offstage, without the stature of the O'Neill characters, the cast looked diminished and ordinary as they pulled on sweaters, talked to one another, and left. I stood in the manner of outsiders, trying to be invisible and look relaxed at the same time. Two men dressed in jeans had a hurried conference about something. The stockier of the two walked to the stage door.

"Did you like it?" the younger one said.

"Who? Me?" It was not a bright remark, because his only other choice was God. The building was deserted except for the two of us. Gus was nowhere to be seen.

"Yes, you, Amanda Pepper."

I was startled until I remembered that Gus had just introduced me to everyone. "You were fine. All of you," I answered, showing my keen critical powers.

He smoked, overtly studying me. He was tall and slender, with dark eyes and a shock of long, thick black hair. His stare made me feel unpleasantly adolescent. He seemed to expect something of me, but I had no idea what. "Got a minute?" he asked. "I really want to talk to you." His words tumbled out and blurred. I recognized him. He was Eddie the mumbler. "Not about the show. Something else. Something important to both of us."

"Do I know you?"

He moved closer. "Not yet." His smile looked pre-packaged, something rehearsed in front of a mirror.

I didn't like him. I didn't like his predictable good looks or his posturing. The sooty smudges beneath his eyes were his single intriguing feature, but I wouldn't have been surprised if they were makeup, put on for effect.

He gave up waiting for me to become his adoring slave. "Look, this is extremely important. You'll have to believe me."

Strangers who tell me what I have to do are only one half notch above strangers who tell me what I dare not do. "I don't mean to be rude," I said, "but we really have nothing to talk about." I turned to look for Gus.

He put his hand on my shoulder. "I don't want to be rude," he mimicked. "Well, you sure as hell are."

I wheeled around and he dropped his hand.

"I'm not asking for a big deal, just for talk. I'm not even asking you to *do* anything about it. Jesus Christ!" His eyes became even darker. He threw down his cigarette and stomped on it. "You act like I'm attacking you or something!"

"I have to go now," I said softly.

Suddenly, his entire posture changed, and he put his hands up in a gesture of surrender. "Sorry," he said. His voice was again low, a mumble. "I—I'm strung out. I scared you, and I didn't mean to." He laughed. "I'm harmless, really."

I didn't believe he was harmless. He was too intense, too much of whatever he was being. Even his new, relaxed self was too much so.

He grinned his fake, cheap grin. "Let's start over, okay? See, I have this kind of sticky legal problem."

"I'm not a lawyer."

"I know that. And it has nothing to do with what I want to ask you, but I don't want to go to the cops if I don't have to. You understand?" He moved closer and put his hand on my upper arm, almost stroking it. I controlled an urge to shudder, and I backed off.

"Eddie? Where the hell are you?" The older man he'd been talking to earlier reappeared through the back door. "I can't see a damn—is that you? Should have known there'd be a pretty face involved. Listen, man, you're holding everything up." He waved in my direction. "Bring her, but get a move on."

Eddie looked uncomfortable. "There's a kind of party," he said finally. "Want to come?"

"I can't. I'm here with Gus."

Eddie looked relieved. "Oh, yeah. Well, too bad. So listen, I have to go now. But I'll be in touch."

The older man propelled Eddie away. "Now I know what keeps you so young," he said as they left.

"So what did you think of the performance?" Gus's voice reached me before he did.

"I didn't understand it."

"Why? She's nervous, but I thought it was a lot better."

"Oh! Sarah's! She's fine, Gus. She's got lots of fire if you can put it in the right place."

He flicked out the last of the auditorium lights, and we walked to the side door. "What performance did you think I meant? What was it you didn't understand?"

"I don't remember," I answered. The only thing I was beginning to understand was the fine art of lying.

Eight

I WORKED AT HOME OVER DINNER, AVERAG-
ing out student quarter-grades. I hate the entire idea
of performance marks, but parents consider them the
merchandise they pay for. The problem is that they
expect the grades to be as inflated as their tuition bills.
I entered a "D" next to Lance Zittsner's name, sighed
for my lost morality, and closed the roll book.

I readied myself for Liza's viewing. I showered and
changed into a severe skirt and blouse I'd bought when
I started teaching and thought I had to look like Miss
Grundy. They were as good as new.

The evening was clear and balmy, and I walked the
few blocks to the funeral home, liking the crisp feel of
early spring. It surrounded me in sweet contrast to all
the spongy, suspect things in my life of late.

The home's entry hall was cavernous, and I was
greeted by an emaciated young man with 1920's
center-parted hair. He led me to a room off the hallway that was filled with the hum of voices and a badly
matched assortment of people.

I recognized several actors and actresses from the
night before. They huddled together, dressed in dark

suits and dresses, all of us looking as if we wore borrowed clothes. The Eddie person stood somewhat
apart, staring at the ceiling. I wondered if he was on
drugs, if that was why he looked both nervous and
drowsy.

Near me stood another cluster of young, very upset
men and women. One of them talked about tenth
grade, about how she and Liza had cut school and
hitchhiked to Atlantic City. Another, very pregnant and
bloated, blew her nose and wiped her eyes.

Nearer to the coffin, I saw Gus and Dr. Havermeyer. My headmaster pulled at his collar and stroked
his belly, waiting to be excused. Helga Putnam stood by
her leader, scowling. She had changed into a dark gray
cardigan.

In the center of the room, sitting near the coffin on a
straight-backed chair, Mrs. Nichols listened to a woman
in rusty black. A few men stood nearby, saying little,
obviously dragged along by their wives.

There were only a few feet between the cluster near
Mrs. Nichols and a threesome in the corner, but the
feet could have been light-years. It was the difference
between what is, what was, and what might have been.

Sissie Bellinger, chic and rail-thin in navy blue and
heavy pearls, formed one pointy edge of the triangle.
She stood next to an impassive, elegantly groomed
Hayden Cole. His mama faced them. She shared her
son's jutting chin, colorless light hair, and solid, tall
frame.

I went to Mrs. Nichols. The flock of women around
her parted expectantly. She clutched my outstretched
hand in both of hers. "Oooh," she moaned loudly,
fresh tears welling over her puffed lower lids. "I still
can't believe it—my baby!" She seemed close to hysteria, keening and wailing and beating her hands with

mine inside them onto her knees. "Have you seen her? Have you seen how beautiful...?" She released me, pushing me toward the open coffin.

Liza did look beautiful. And unfamiliar. With no animation, no drama, with her jet hair haloing her still face, with the bruise I could never forget cosmetically hidden, she looked like a sleeping child and no one I had ever known. Even so, the sight was terrible, and I moved my eyes away over it quickly, trying to leave no imprints.

Mrs. Nichols screamed, "Liza! My Liza!"

I turned away, feeling like a voyeur to so much naked pain. Gus's sympathetic face greeted me. Then I saw Sissie staring incredulously at Mrs. Nichols, and beside her, Mrs. Cole and her ramrod back. They had no qualms about watching and silently condemning Mrs. Nichols's misery.

Main Line ladies' upper lips were genetically stiff, and only genteel sounds could squeeze through them. Mrs. Nichols, made only of flesh, sounded primitive and frightening.

"Pray for Liza," the women around Mrs. Nichols crooned, patting her shoulders and clucking until the heavy, choking sobs gradually stopped. The bereaved turned into a bulky woman of stone, staring blindly ahead. "Thank you for coming," she said flatly.

The circle of women closed in on her and filled the room's sudden silence with more comforting noises.

"Mrs. Cole would like to meet you," Gus said. I followed him into the corner.

"Ah," Mrs. Cole said, shaking my hand vigorously. "Amanda Pepper, the one who... It must be so difficult for you, dear. So trying. We have thought of you constantly during this dreadful time."

Hayden, who had definitely thought about me, stood

a bit behind his mother, avoiding me as much as he could.

Sissie, who had also thought about me—if actual thoughts passed between her jet streams of observations—fidgeted, but didn't interrupt the older woman.

"Knowing Liza so intimately," Mrs. Cole added.

"Well, actually, I didn't," I began.

"Miss Pepper prefers to consider herself as merely an acquaintance of Liza's," Hayden said dryly.

"To lose your dear friend," Mrs. Cole continued, undeterred, "to lose a confidante, a girlhood companion. Oh, when I was your age, how terrible it would have been."

I had a vision of girls in organdy ruffles, whispering innocent secrets in a garden of phlox, and wondered what her images could possibly have to do with me. I didn't consider my stage in life "girlhood," either, but the woman was nodding agreement with her own statements, and I didn't think a discussion of semantics was appropriate.

"Isn't it terrible?" she said directly to me.

"Yes," I said, not certain what, precisely, I was agreeing to.

"And to have to speak with the police, to be questioned. I find it trying. They have no sense of propriety. No manners. The most brash young man came to our house. I refused to speak to him after a time. Don't you agree? Didn't you?"

Hayden eyed me suspiciously. Sissie paced back and forth, hovering like a vulture. And Mrs. Cole examined me intently. I knew I was being tested, and for some reason, I wanted to pass, or at least stay in the running. "I talked to them, but I didn't have anything much to say. I don't know anything."

Hayden's mouth turned down with distaste.

"I never had a daughter," Mrs. Cole said, off on a side trail of her own. "I had such hopes, such hopes."

Sissie, who had all the necessary qualifications for the newly vacated position of Cole daughter, took this opportunity to reach over and pat the older woman's arm. Mrs. Cole didn't seem to notice.

I searched for a graceful out. Gus was no help, lounging against the nearby wall. I looked around. Near the door I saw a familiar tall figure, a brash young policeman with blue eyes that circled the room, noting whatever it was he was paid to note. He noted me, we shifted our heads slightly to acknowledge each other, and then Mrs. Cole began again.

"I would like to talk with you," she said. "I want to know more about poor, dear Liza, and you knew her best."

"But really, I didn't." It is not seemly to speak, or probably to think, ill of the dead, and it's certainly futile to resent them, but Liza's lies had outlived her and were twisting my life around. I wasted a few moments dealing with lots of directionless anger. "Certainly," I insisted, "your son knew her a great deal better than I did."

"I think we should leave, Mother," her son said. He glanced at his watch and looked displeased. "I've already postponed the meeting."

"Oh, Hayden!" Mrs. Cole smiled at him. "You're so busy all the time!" She looked at me. "He's so concerned about helping others. The geriatric groups. The handicapped, and on and on." She leaned close. "My son is a good man, Miss Pepper. Thinks and does only what is good. That's why it's important he become senator."

"We must say good-night to Mrs. Nichols," Hayden said impatiently, taking his mother's elbow. "And to you, Miss Pepper."

Gus left his post by the wall when the Coles and Sissie were out of earshot. "Ugly people, aren't they?" he said. "And Liza was waltzing right into their arms."

Not ugly. But odd, most definitely. Especially odd about me. Why me? What was it everybody, including Gus, thought I knew? And what would convince them all that I didn't?

"Gus, we should go now." Sarah Halvorsen's voice was low but emphatic. She stood in front of us, along with several others of the company.

"All right," Gus said, "let's make our farewells." He merged into the little knot of actors moving toward Mrs. Nichols.

I walked over to the crowd and waited my turn. Mrs. Cole's broad back was in front of me. She, her son, and Sissie waited stolidly in silence. They seemed withdrawn from the scene and the people around them.

"Amanda Pepper. I knew we'd meet again soon." Eddie stood close to me, smiling, looking almost innocent and boyish.

Mrs. Nichols sobbed in the background, her cries muffled by the people around her.

"Look," Eddie said, "it's because you're the one who found—"

I could not bear hearing that again. Of all the careers and claims to fame I'd ever imagined, none had been based on being "the one who found the body." The disgust on my face must have been obvious.

"Don't get mad again," he said. "There's something we have to talk about."

"I don't know anything."

"I think I do," he said. He rolled an unlit cigarette in

his hand, waiting to get outside and light it. His long fingers trembled. The circles under his eyes were now a frightening purple.

"Why tell me?" I asked. "Why not tell the police?" I kept my voice low and calm.

"I can't. I've got enough hassles with the law already, and I can't. Besides, until I talk to you, I'm not one hundred percent sure if what I know is important." He reached out and clasped my wrist. "Trust me," he said.

"Why?"

We were moving closer to Mrs. Nichols, pushed forward by the crowd. "You were the last to see her," he said. "Well, almost. You were one in the middle. And see, I think—"

"Shh," I said because his voice was becoming reedy with urgency, and I didn't think this was an appropriate conversation for the mournful, subdued setting.

"Did she tell you about it?" he said, whispering now.

"About what?"

"About...about her news?"

"She didn't tell me anything."

He looked surprised. "She didn't?" He released my wrist and rubbed his hand over his bruised-looking eyes. They seemed much older than the rest of him. "I was sure she did. This is driving me up the wall. I tried to see you the other night. Waited near your house, but when I finally got the nerve to approach you, you screamed. Then a car came, and I—"

"It was you!" I momentarily forgot to monitor my voice, and Eddie shushed me now.

"I didn't mean to frighten you," he said. "I'm telling you, I was scared myself. I didn't know you. But I had to talk to you, alone."

"Go to the police, Eddie," I repeated. "I don't know anything. She didn't tell me anything. I swear it."

"Listen," he whispered urgently as I moved forward. "Listen to me. Talk to me."

"I am."

"No. Not here."

I shook my head.

"Listen, you don't think I did it, do you? Why would I hurt her?"

"Why would anybody? But somebody did."

"Okay. Talk to me someplace you won't be scared. I have to go to rehearsal after this. How about tomorrow? After the funeral, in public. Outside. That could be private and still safe enough for you."

I shrugged.

"It's a deal. And then, if you think I should, I swear I'll go to the police."

"Listen, Eddie, you're not making a whole lot of sense."

"I will, after we talk."

The Coles and Sissie turned to leave, having completed stiff farewells to Mrs. Nichols.

Eddie gave them a cursory nod, said a quick "tomorrow" to me, and left the room.

"Miss Pepper," Mrs. Cole said, "I meant it about wanting to spend time with you. That was not mere social pleasantry."

"Mother Cole," Sissie said, obviously pushing for daughterly status, "we must rush." Her voice was at its most cultivated, and it floated and lounged above the earthy sounds of the masses below it.

When it was my turn, Mrs. Nichols accepted my words passively.

At the doorway, C. K. Mackenzie monitored the room with singular apathy. He yawned as I approached him, then belatedly covered his mouth with his hand. "Feelin' all right tonight?" he said softly

when I was near. "No more hysteria? Haven't heard
from you, so I figured you were still intact."

"I'm fine. And what brings you here?"

"I'm supposed to do this sort of thing. In movies,
detectives always appear at funerals, viewings, you
know. They experience epiphanies."

"And have you?"

"Not even a minor truth became obvious. I'm ready
to drop, anyway."

I believed him. His eyes, half shut, had lost their
wattage. His normal slouch was exaggerated, drooping
dangerously near to a crawl.

"You leavin' too?" he asked.

We nodded farewell to the slick funeral director.
"I'm doing the right things," C.K. muttered as we
walked. "I run around and collect things that don't
add up. I sit with Ray and try to make it add up anyway. I go back and forth to the Playhouse, her modeling agency, the bastions of the rich—"

"I gathered as much," I said. "Everybody I meet
seems to be spending time with you on a daily basis."

"We read reports and talk," he droned on, barely ac-
knowledging me. "And nothing. I came here tonight,
studied the list of visitors, carefully scrutinized every-
thin', and instead of revelation, I get fatigue." We were
down on the sidewalk. "Want a lift?"

His car, for no apparent reason, smelled of popcorn.

"Maybe it's no good being officially labeled 'detective,'" I said. "You go around trying to force people to
tell you things. They clam up. But I stand still, knowing zilch, and people come on to me, force-feeding me
tidbits. Maybe I find out more than you do."

I thought that'd tantalize him, but he was less than
intrigued. He scratched his head and stared at his igni-
tion key. "Like that dark-haired fellow?" he finally

said. "Saw some heavy action between you two. He doesn't seem your type, though." Mackenzie yawned and began driving, very slowly.

I almost asked Mackenzie which parts of my household inventory made him deduce what my type might be. But he was right; Eddie wasn't my type, and as fascinating as it is hearing myself described, I was not the topic at hand. "Eddie, that dark-haired fellow, is an actor. At the Playhouse. He wants to talk to me about Liza."

"I know who he is. I talked to him. He isn't a suspect. He was working all day Monday. He's clean. And I think he was coming on to you in a kind of creepy way, considerin' the circumstances."

"He has something he wants to say. To me. Not to the police."

"I'll just bet. And who could blame him for his preference?" We waited for a light to change. Mackenzie rested his head on the steering wheel.

"About Liza. He wants to talk about Liza."

This time my somnolent driver attempted to smother his yawn by holding his lips together. He looked like a blowfish.

"I'm serious, Mackenzie," I said. "And you're barely listening. This could be important stuff. Also," I said, forcefully, so that it would penetrate his stupor, "Sissie Bellinger has twice been at me, asking what Liza said, what I know."

"Uh-huh," he said, barely moving his mouth. "People love firsthand tellings. That's what sells all those magazines in the supermarket, you know?"

"It's more than that. Hayden Cole is behaving suspiciously. He practically kidnapped me yesterday. I forgot to tell you."

"Forgot?" Mackenzie shook his head. "Forgot a kidnapping?"

"Well, it was almost one. He made me ride around with him, and he questioned me."

"Made you? Forced you? Dragged you? Hit you?"

"Well, his man, this Haskell creep, yanked me."

"And Hayden? What did he do?"

"He, ah, he told him to stop."

"Wow," Mackenzie said; then he yawned again.

I sat up straight for my final offering, hoping it would trigger some sympathetic response.

"Then listen to this one, C.K. Hayden's mother followed it up by telling me that her little boy wouldn't hurt a fly and that he'd better become senator because he's all goodness and light. She's weird."

"Yeah," he agreed. "And she told me all that, too, even though I am an official detective. He was a good little boy. Citizenship award every year. Perfect attendance record. Dean's list at Franklin and Marshall. Right fraternity, right—"

"Doesn't it make you suspicious? Why is she pouring his innocence all over you? I mean, my brother-in-law was in the same right fraternity at F&M as Cole was, but I don't rush around making sure you know that. What's its relevance? Any of it?"

But he was on a roll, and as soon as my interruption ended, he resumed his sentence. "...law firm. Right father. Right mother. Nice baby, nice boy, nice man..."

Mackenzie was driving five miles an hour. He even lacked the energy to press on the gas pedal.

"It's the way she said it that's important, Mackenzie! Wake up! Why should she talk to me that way?"

Have you ever noticed how we rush to fill vacuums?

Energy vacuums included? As if there's a base level that must be maintained at all costs. So the lower-keyed Mackenzie got, the more manic and expressive I became, just so there'd be evidence of life in the car. I gesticulated, I emphasized, I trilled, I pleaded. "Hayden quizzes me, Mama prompts me," I said. "Isn't it all obvious? What's his alibi for Monday? Did you check it out?"

He stopped in midyawn. His ego was obviously still hearty. "What kind of question is that? Of course I did. He was with some dumb—the Thursday Club. Except they meet Mondays. Late breakfast, then a conference with his campaign manager."

We were finally in front of my house. C.K. put the car into neutral and rubbed his eyes.

"Yes, but I mean *really* check. Was he with other people every single minute? And wouldn't they cover for him, anyway? As his campaign manager would, wouldn't he? Were there any breaks in time, long enough to get to my house?" I felt inspired, considered myself one of the great orators. My honeyed words, my persuasive powers, would convince the slow-witted detective.

He stared at me, his mouth half-open.

"Look!" I said, eyebrows rising to convey the message. "The suburban clique is too worried—look how hard they're pushing me! If you really go over his schedule Monday, minute by minute—and Sissie's, too—you might find something."

"My, oh, my," he said. "Havin' fun, aren't you? Look at you now! Perky little lady sleuth. Nancy Drew's all grown up."

I shriveled and tumbled from my podium. "I resent that."

"Hold on, now. I have been on this for four straight

days with almost no sleep. There's a lot of pressure you don't know about, family bein' so prominent and all. But I know my business. I'm good at it. Your business is teachin' English. You're good at that. But your part of my business is over. Stay out. I appreciate your good intentions, but this is my job." He ran out of steam.

"Good night," I said stiffly, getting out of the car. "Do get some sleep. It's supposed to rejuvenate brain cells."

"I'll wait till you're inside," he said, sagging over the steering wheel. "I'll see you tomorrow at the funeral. All us detectives go to those things, too."

I went into my house, fuming over the way my tax dollars were being wasted on that dimwit. I wondered how and why I had ever, even for a moment, found him the least bit appealing.

Nine

I OVERSLEPT, WAKING IN TIME TO DO NO more than ready myself for the funeral. I straggled downstairs to make coffee, then shuffled back up, cup in hand, complimenting myself for mastering coffee without cigarettes for six straight days, and they hadn't been the easiest of days.

This one wasn't going to be any easier. I brushed my teeth carefully, concentrating on them, not the impending funeral. I'd seen death firsthand now, seen it on my living room floor. But I'd blurred it, pushed it as far away as I could all week, pretending it could be solved and sponged from my life. Last night I'd turned away from Mrs. Nichols's grief and what it represented. Today, it would be solemnized and ritualized, and I would have to face it.

But later. Meanwhile, there were less significant problems to consider. Mackenzie wasn't really insignificant yet, but his insufferable behavior had certainly reduced his stature. I would have to face him, too, but that was a face I could prepare. I practiced cold and haughty expressions in the bathroom mirror. The cat

jumped up and watched me have a significant inter-
change with my reflection.

"Can't talk, Mackenzie," I murmured. "Must run
now. Back to my real life, you know." And of course,
my very tone would remind him that I am an academic,
a civilized woman whose life is not compatible with a
flatfoot's. "Good luck and good-bye, Mackenzie!"

The cat stopped in midwash. "I said Mackenzie, not
Macavity, you dumb beast." He resumed his toilette.

"Or," I mumbled, dental floss between my teeth, "call
me if you ever need help again, Mackenzie. Eddie's
information really broke open this case, didn't it,
though?"

I hoped it did. All I knew about Eddie was that he
was a two-bit player in a semiprofessional group of
actors, an intense, scared rabbit who followed me, then
ran away. I didn't even know his full name.

Finding that out intrigued me more than dental hy-
giene. I put down the flosser, risking gum disease.
Maybe my accumulated plaque would bring me to an
interesting, single, periodontist. It would please my
mother.

I went to find the playbill.

It was still next to the bedroom telephone. I scanned
it while I put on panty hose. No Eddie in the starring
roles. Then I found it. He gave himself his full Edward, which seemed much too formal for his style. Edward Bayer. One of the minor players, part of the
team of dull names.

I pulled on a navy turtleneck dress before it hit me.
Before I heard it, instead of just seeing it.

"Edward Bayer," I said out loud, stunned. "Edward
Bear." The real, the honest-to-Milne-given name of
Winnie the Pooh.

I whirred around my room, pulling shoes out of the closet, running a comb through my hair, slapping appropriate, I hoped, makeup on my face. "Thank you, niece Karen, for endless evenings with that bear. I'll share my good citizenship award with you."

I glanced at the playbill again, then turned it over. Mackenzie's various phone numbers, written in firmly blockish characters, faced me. Given his energy level last night, I was certain he hadn't rushed out at dawn to sniff for clues.

"Take that, Mackenzie," I said, punching my index finger into his telephone number. "So the big professional who knows his business examined lists of names, talked to everybody, and still found nothing. So I'm just an English teacher who should stop playing sleuth, am I?" I reached for the telephone.

Then I paused. Why waste my golden moment of triumph on the phone? I'd see him in less than an hour. And I wanted to see him. Wanted to watch his sleepy eyes open in wonder. Wanted to wait patiently while he searched for humble, apologetic words. I deserved to see it firsthand.

I practiced gloating while I walked to my car. A lot of things made sense now. Eddie was the reason for Liza's lies about staying with me. She used them for both her mother and Hayden.

Eddie had been with her Sunday night. After the Playhouse performance. He called me the one in the middle. After him. Before the killer.

But why not Edward the Bear as killer?

I considered Eddie as a potential menace as I drove. He could be afraid, like all the others, that Liza had told me something important. But I couldn't see the danger in talking to him at the cemetery, in full view of other people. He was a coward at heart. He wouldn't do anything there. And for a coward to come forward that way, to promise to go to the police, which frightened him, must mean he had something important to say.

I was one of the first to arrive at the funeral home, and I was ushered to a seat near the front of the chapel. I looked around at the sprinkling of faces. Some were familiar. The pregnant high school friend was there, next to a beefy young man. Sarah Halvorsen sat alone, stiff and withdrawn.

"Early, aren't we?" a familiar voice said. Sissie wore something dark and silky that whispered along with her as she slid in next to me. "Not many here. Why? Maybe too early, is all. Or she wasn't as popular as she liked to..." I was not in the mood, never had been, for the woman's soliloquy, but there was no polite exit.

"Exhausted," she said, "rushing all the time. Too much, too much. Extra rehearsals, running around, the fair tomorrow night. And of course, I am still Petey's mother."

I have nothing firsthand to say about mothering, so I nodded and stayed silent. Sissie didn't mind.

"Wherever are the Coles?" She glanced at her watch, and as if on cue, they entered, seating themselves across the aisle. Sissie waved. Hayden finally noticed, smiled, and stayed put.

"Poor man's going through hell," Sissie whispered. "I try my best to ease the pressure, poor Hay, but..." She shook her head and paused, surprising me while she waited for a response.

"You're very close, aren't you?" I murmured, looking around. Where was Eddie?

"Close? Almost family. Our parents had Sunday

dinners together before we were born. Spent summers at Cape May together, celebrated holidays, were law partners..."

Sissie switched gears to her theater woes. "Really nervous about Sarah. Stick of wood. Wish the other hadn't taken the country thing, but who knew? Could have finished the run and gone away. Said she would. Who could have known?"

It did no good to pay attention to her. My mind hopped back over her words, trying to sort them out. "The other" shouldn't have taken that role, but then who could have finished the run and gone away? Not that same other. Liza? Liza had said she'd go away? "Who do you mean..." I began, but I gave up. Sissie wouldn't clarify anything. She was good at talking, not at saying anything. I returned to my increasingly difficult search for Eddie's dark head. The pews were filling with neighbors, actors, a sprinkle of polished faces that must have been from the modeling agency, and a group of well-dressed men who came up to Hayden before finding seats.

He greeted them politely, but after they'd moved off, he sat rigidly, running his hand across his collar, brushing imaginary specks off his lapel. His mother sat next to him like a monument.

The chapel became so full I couldn't see more than a row or two behind me. I couldn't even find Mackenzie, who was surely slouching in a rear pew.

A swell of solemn music announced the service. I felt a lurch of fear, a desire to run away.

"They asked Hayden to give the eulogy. Poor taste, I think. Declined, of course," Sissie whispered.

I tensed up, afraid of what I was going to hear, of what I was going to have to learn, once and for all. But I needn't have worried. The minister had no real knowledge of Liza, and his all-purpose, impersonal words were vague and meaningless, filled with tributes to the life hereafter and laments for those cut down before their time.

They didn't penetrate the wall around my emotions. I was safe in my fortress, and I relaxed a little.

Afterward, we filed out slowly. I had to wait for all those behind me to leave, and by the time I edged out into the daylight, only a handful of people were around. A line of filled cars waited to leave for the cemetery.

"Oh, Miss Pepper! Can I ride with you? Please? I don't have a car." It was Stacy Felkin, the student who had idolized Liza. Her mascara again smeary, she blew her nose and looked up at me. "The other kids left already. They forgot about me."

"Of course," I said. Who could deny her passage? It wasn't far from the truth to say that she was Liza's one true mourner. "I'm parked around the corner."

"Mornin'," a voice drawled. "Or afternoon, to be precise." His smile was open and guileless, his blue eyes bright. It became difficult envisioning him as the humbled wreck of my morning fantasies.

"Hello," I said coolly. I introduced the detective and the student.

"I saw him at school," Stacy said, blowing her nose again.

"Are you more rested today?" I asked C.K. It was hard to tell with this man.

"Ah, yes," he said with another smile. "Slept twelve hours. I feel great. You ladies want a lift to the cemetery? My car's right here."

Stacy paused in her attempt to remove the smudges around her eyes. "You'd drive us?" she said, ready to adopt another hero on the spot. I didn't want to be

around to see how she'd adapt to Mackenzie's shuffling, drawling style.

If the aroma of popcorn was still in the car, it was
smothered by Stacy's perfume, a musky scent reminiscent of Liza's. We drove in silence through gray city
streets and then into and through the dull-green park
ringing the city.

Stacy's pocketbook was drilling a large cavity in my
hipbone. I pulled it out from between us and handed
it to her. "Pretty bag," I murmured.

She regarded it lovingly. "It's like the one Miss Nichols carried. Almost."

With every breath I inhaled a Stacy-mutated varia-
tion of Liza's scent. Stacy's hair was a scraggly version
of Liza's mane. Stacy's peasant dress imitated one of
Liza's favorite costumes.

"And see what my mother gave me for my birthday?" Stacy fumbled at her neck. She held up a heart-
shaped locket. "I asked for it three months ago. It's
like Miss Nichols's. Almost."

Mackenzie maneuvered the car through the cemetery gates. The gravesite wasn't far away. I could see a
group clustered around it, but no Eddie.

"I see the other kids, Miss Pepper," Stacy whispered,
although we weren't close to the grave yet. "I can get a
ride home from them. Thanks, sir."

Mackenzie nodded, and she swished off. "Pepper?"
he said, clearing his throat. "I, er, spent the morning
going over Cole's schedule for last Monday again." He
became engrossed in a cloud formation above us.

I couldn't catch his eye.

"Hey there, big fellow," I finally said. "Was that by
any chance an apology? Are you suggesting that you're
not a full-time, supercilious, smug, self-satisfied—"

"I'm sayin' I'm sorry. What are you sayin'?"

"That I accept your apology." I was sufficiently touched to decide to tell him about Eddie without fanfare. "Listen, this morning, I—"

"Shh," he said, gesturing toward the grave. "They're starting."

The circle made room for me, although I didn't want it. I stared at Liza's dark coffin, heard the minister's ritualized words. This time, it didn't matter what he said. The coffin, the raw oblong cut in the earth, were eloquent in their silence.

And then, at some point, it was over and Mackenzie, with the gentlest of touches, guided me back to his car.

I couldn't speak. There seemed nothing worth saying, nothing comparable to the lesson just learned.

Mackenzie drove until he found a diner near the edge of the city.

"Coffee?" he asked, and I shrugged, then nodded.

When the steamy mugs arrived, when the clatter of dishes and murmur of voices pushed me back into the living, I finally found my voice again. "It got to me," I said.

He nodded, and I knew then that it got to him, too, over and over again.

"How can you stand it?" I demanded, half-angry, as if he created the messes he lived with. "How can you face a lifetime of it?"

"I don't know that I will. I started out a sociology major at Rice. Taking criminology courses now." He shrugged and fiddled with his coffee spoon, made patterns on the paper placemat with its tip. "Maybe I'll go into something less concrete than this, theorize about the causes of crime, work in a lab and analyze things. I'm not sure. Or law. I think about that, too. It's the other end of the continuum. This seemed a good starting point, though...." He didn't seem altogether comfortable with his vague future, and he wound up staring out the thick window beside him. "Spring's gone all to hell again," he said. "Looks like a bad black-and-white photo. No contrasts. No bright whites, just grainy gray."

I looked out the foggy window along with him. "Landscape painters must save money around here," I said, hoping to pull us both back onto more familiar ground, even if it was as antagonists again. "They only have to buy black and white paint. Can you imagine the history of art if, say, Renoir had been born a Phila-delphian?"

"Or van Gogh," Mackenzie said, the ghost of a twin-kle back in his eye. "Painting this place. The gray-silver diner on its gray-white concrete blocks. Under a pale gray sky, above blacktop. He'd have cut off his hands, not his ear. But that brings us back to violence, doesn't it? Isn't there something else?"

"Yes. Yes, there is." It was violence-related, or vio-lence-born, I guess, but that needn't be said. Macken-zie had long since redeemed himself, and I wasn't going to bludgeon him with my revelation, just present it as a gift. "Big news, Mackenzie," I said. "I know who Winnie the Pooh is."

"I'm right proud of you. But so do I. And I know about Christopher Robin and Tigger as well."

"No—Liza's bear. Her Winnie. The charm, re-member? That guy last night, Eddie Bayer, the actor. Edward Bear is Winnie the Pooh's real name. Not only that, but Eddie Bayer was the person outside my house Tuesday night, but I scared him, he scared me, and you scared us both." I sat back and waited for the round of applause and the expression of gratitude.

Instead, Mackenzie plonked down his coffee cup. "You knew this, but you didn't bother to tell me?"

"I didn't know about the name until I was getting dressed today. Then I put two and two together."

He didn't really have to applaud, but I certainly deserved a nod of approbation.

"And you didn't say anything till now?"

"When could I? Stacy was in the car, and—"

"That lumpy little girl's some kind of spy? Or do you think she's our killer?"

"It didn't feel right. Not then. Also, I was supposed to talk to Eddie at the cemetery. I didn't want you to interfere. I was positive—I still am—that he knows something."

"I'd rather not believe this. The first new link, the first maybe something, and you're too miffed to share it. You were supposed to meet him there today?"

"I told you last night. I said he wanted to talk to me."

"The way you said it, I didn't think—"

"Mackenzie, you didn't think at all last night. And what you did instead was enough to shut anybody up. In fact, you *told* me to stop playing Nancy Drew."

"All right!" He drained his cup, bit his bottom lip, and stood up. "Let's find him." He put change on the Formica table.

"He doesn't want to see *us*. Certainly not the police. He's nervous about something." I stood on tiptoe, almost, oddly annoyed that he still towered above me.

"He's nervous? So am I. Why wasn't he there today?" Mackenzie's entire tempo had changed. He moved briskly, paid the cashier, pushed through the revolving door, and even spoke double-time. I had difficulty following him.

"He didn't do it," I said when I caught up. "Why should you think he did it?"

"I don't. I told you he was working Monday. But now that I know who he is, what his relationship is—"

"Thanks to me," I said, but he ignored me. I was pretty sure I wasn't going to get a citizen's citation out of this.

"He probably does know something. Certainly more than anybody else so far. I'm tired of this case. Tired of interesting gossip that adds up to zero. Come on."

I sat quietly on my side of the car. C. K. Mackenzie and I probably had clashing biorhythm charts. Something was consistently and badly out of synch between us. If I offered ideas, I was playing girl detective. If I didn't, I was withholding information. Ours was destined to be the shortest nonrelationship on record.

He backed out of the space and then jammed on the brakes. "Where the hell am I going? Where does he live?" He pulled out his pathetic notebook and thumbed through it. "Okay. West Philly. Not too far."

"Let me explain myself," he said after a while, his voice too conspicuously patient. "I don't like being called a supercilious, smug, what have you. But I can't close a case because somebody's mama is overly enamored of her sonny boy. Or because somebody almost, not really, kidnaps you so nicely that it slips your mind for a day. So I don't spend a whole lot of time on that kind of intellectual exercise."

"I don't see what you're—"

"I'm still explainin'! Because, on the other hand, I am intensely interested in reality. Like how to decipher the name of a lover. Like somebody missin' an appointment he took trouble to set up. Those are real things."

I shrugged and slumped as deeply as the safety belt would allow.

"And another real thing is a murder." He pronounced it "murdah," so I knew his stress level was way up, and his practice at speaking like a native was meaningless. "Murdah is real. And this one was strictly amateur stuff—a first, desperate impulse, ah believe. So it could be anybody, but once they've taken that step, what's to stop the next one? So that's real, too. And dangerous. And not a game at all. You could get hurt real bad messin' with it. Don't you see the difference?"

"Not too well, obviously."

He glanced over at me. "Oh, dammit, don't look like that. Maybe I'm not bein' fair. You're new to all this. And, well, thanks. That was clever of you, the bear. I never would have caught on. Neither would Ray or anybody else on the case."

"I'm sorry I waited to tell you about Eddie," I said softly. It was hard saying any more. That primitive center of me still believed that saying things made them possible, and silence kept them from happening. But I forced myself ahead. "Do you think it's going to make some kind of difference? To anybody?"

"I sincerely hope not" was all he'd say. The man was not comforting, but he was honest.

Ten

"LIZA LIKED VARIETY IN MEN, DIDN'T SHE?"
Mackenzie said, chitchatting his way through the traffic
and tension. "Bayer is, in case you hadn't noticed,
somewhat different from Cole. From lawyer-legislator
to baker's assistant, whatever that might be."

"That's it!"

"What? What's what?"

"Listen, Mackenzie, I have something to say. But I
don't know whether you'll consider it reality or speculation, and I don't feel like messing with you again.
Could I be granted immunity to bumble around?"

"You're a mean woman, Peppah."

"I take it that means I may proceed. I'm sure Liza
was with Eddie Sunday night after the show. But I
couldn't understand why she left so early. Except that
bakeries tool up at dawn. That explains what she was
doing wandering toward town at daybreak."

Mackenzie smiled. "See? I'm not shoutin' or stomp-
in' on you."

"You're not congratulating me, either."

"Congratulations," he said, after a pause.

We passed the blitz-blocks, the section of the City of

Brotherly Love that had undergone urban renewal by police bombing. The new houses, looking a little embarrassed, were solid and resolutely middle-class. Also, I thought, a little more fortresslike than their unhappy predecessors.

We moved on and came to an area that looked as if it, too, had been bombed but never rehabilitated. Two houses in the row had boarded-up windows, and almost all of them had black spray-paint graffiti that made them look trapped in enormous nets. I have a hard time with people who call this form of vandalism art.

"I'm deputizin' you," Mackenzie said, surprising me. I tried to look nonchalant about his change of heart, to avoid dragging Nancy Drew's name into our conversation again.

Mackenzie parked across the street from Eddie's address. "Find out what he wants to say. Simple enough?"

I stared at the house. Its green porch railing was missing half its spokes. The steps were swaybacked and the patch of lawn in front was bald, except for discarded trash.

"This is the address he gave me," Mackenzie said. "I'll wait ten minutes. Then I'm comin' in to talk to him."

My deal had been to talk to Eddie at the cemetery, not behind walls in a rackety house. But I didn't want to blow my new and shaky partnership with Mackenzie, or to reveal my true core of cowardice. I walked up the wooden steps, carefully testing for solid portions before putting down weight.

I wasn't sure if the bell worked. In any case, nobody answered it. I knocked and waited, then knocked again. No answer. I did an extravagant pantomime asking whether I should wait, and Mackenzie gave me a thumbs-up sign from the car.

I sat down on the top step. To the left and right of me, porches echoed, and I tried to envision a warm summer night, with the whole block socializing in front of their houses. I think we lost a lot when we chucked porches. A patio or deck is not the same thing at all.

Two small children, one dark, one fair, both dirty, ran toward my steps. "You *have* to share!" the boy, the smaller of the two, screamed. "*Mommy said!*"

The woman tagging behind them was not a testimonial to the joys of motherhood. I would think of her when next I heard the ticks of my biological time clock. She looked both young and old, exhausted in both cases. Her light brown hair was pulled back into a nondescript knot, and her mouth, unmade, scowled. "Don't you make trouble," she said as she approached. "I warned you, Doreen." Her eyes were directed to the pavement, not the child she addressed.

"Doreen's chewing it all! It's not fair!"

"I'll give you fair," the woman muttered; then she stopped, like a weary horse at its destination. She finally noticed me. "You looking for me?"

"Well, actually, I was looking for Eddie Bayer. He lives here, doesn't he?"

"Not so you'd notice. Why? What's it to you?" She backed up a pace and stared at me, her hands on her hips. "Go away," she said. I guess I flunked inspection.

"But I—"

"Look, lady, I don't know what story he told you. He's got one for everybody. But you aren't going to find him here. He's gone."

"You're . . . ?"

"Catherine Bayer."

"His . . . his wife?"

"Sort of." She shrugged. "He never mentions me, does he? Or them." She jerked her head in the direction of the children, who faced each other in a standoff. "So go away, lady. I don't want to know about you. I don't want my kids to know about you. I don't need your troubles. I got enough already." She started up the steps, walking like a much heavier woman, pausing next to where I stood. "I didn't think you were his type. They're usually delicate. Like I was."

"It isn't like that," I said. "I'm ... with the police."

Mrs. Bayer visibly stiffened and clutched her bag of groceries closer. "The police? I told him I called them, but I didn't. Not really. I was angry; I wanted to—" Her pale skin turned yellow. "Wait. He's in trouble. Sweet Jesus, what is it now? I knew it. The way he was, I knew it."

"He isn't. I just want to talk to him."

The little boy belted his sister. "You chewed it all!" he bellowed.

"Listen, lady," Catherine Bayer said, "I haven't seen him in days."

"He gave us this address."

"I don't know why. He's been gone awhile."

I gestured across the street. Mackenzie waved laconically.

"My partner. Detective Mackenzie," I said quietly.

She looked back at the car, then at me. "Get up here!" she shouted at her children. "Eddie's near Haverford and City Line. Some Jewish bakery. He's been there since he lost his last job. Lives on top of the place. I don't know the address, but it's easy to find when you have to, and I should know."

"She *swallowed* it!" the boy screamed. "It's all gone!"

Catherine Bayer walked heavily to her daughter and smacked her midstride. Then, saying nothing, she unlocked her front door and went in. I assumed this was farewell.

"City Line, near Haverford," I told Mackenzie.

We left the dismal street. "What was that? His mailing address?"

"Maybe he expects to move back in soon." I filled Mackenzie in as we plowed slowly through the Friday backwash of traffic. The transit strike had passed from being a threat into a reality. We crept along, circling a construction site decorated with signs heralding urban progress. There was not, however, a workman in sight.

Finally, between a window of yellowing brassieres and one bright with record albums, we spotted a bakery.

"All right," Mackenzie said, once more parking across the street. "Let's try again."

"The store looks closed," I said. "There's a sign."

Mackenzie rolled down his window and we both deciphered the hand-lettered cardboard sign. "Closed for the holidays. Happy Passover," we finally made out. Mackenzie sighed. "That, alas, is not the information we require."

"Okay, I'll be right back." I walked across the busy street at the first break in traffic and studied the row of buildings. The entrance to the apartment above the store was inside a short alleyway. The street-level door was unlocked. I climbed a long, dark flight of stairs and knocked at his door.

"Eddie? It's Amanda Pepper." I pressed his bell, but I couldn't hear any ringing inside. I pressed it again. Both his addresses had broken doorbells.

I tried the knob, and the door opened. "Eddie?" I called, poking my head halfway inside. "Eddie, it's Mandy Pepper. Can I come in?"

There was still no answer. But I could see a sliver of the room. A tilted dresser, one leg cracked, had every drawer open, contents spilled halfway out. Nearby I saw the edge of a mattress with a madras throw pulled off and a sheet crumpled on top of it. There were papers and photographs on the bare floor.

I hadn't expected a decorator's dream, but I'm not so sexist that I think every bachelor's apartment looks like Dante's fifth circle of hell. I closed the door and bounded down the stairs and across the street.

"Mackenzie, could you come up?"

"Something wrong?"

He opened the door before I could answer and followed me across the street and up the stairs.

"The door's unlocked," I said, whispering now.

The entire room was in the same chaotic state as the sliver I'd seen.

"Dammit," C.K. said. "Dammit all to hell."

He walked around the living room quietly and quickly, not touching anything. There was very little to have made such a mess. But the mattress was off the bed-couch, a rocking chair was upended, and the chest of drawers had been ransacked.

To one side, a narrow corridor led to a room empty of everything except a thick parka on the floor and a pair of skis propped against the wall.

Farther down the hall, a greenish light poured out from the kitchen.

"Sweet Mother of God," Mackenzie said. I was too close behind him to stop, to turn and run away, and I saw it. I tried to look at the room instead, at the translucent lime curtain at the window, the brick wall on the horizon beyond it, the tiny white kitchen table.

"He's dead," Mackenzie said, turning away. "Don't

look." But I already had. He was slumped over the table, near an overturned cup. A brown coffee stain led to Eddie's head.

There was something wrong with the side of Eddie's face on the table. It was discolored, almost shiny and taut. His hair was wrong, too, matted and flat near the nape of his neck. Then I realized that the brown stain on his neck and shirt wasn't coffee. He had been burned. I swayed in place, paralyzed.

From a very far distance, I watched Mackenzie survey the ugly green kitchen, the sink full of dirty dishes, the old gas stove, the refrigerator with the drip pan. Then he turned back to me. "Enough," he said, leading me out of the room. He found a phone under the madras spread and dialed headquarters.

He gestured for me to leave as he spoke, and I managed to move my feet a few paces unassisted, but I was afraid to go far, and I stayed on the landing, with the door open. He spoke for a while, but my cloudy mind picked up only the word "homicide."

I was not surprised, but I was sickened. I gagged, held my stomach, and took deep breaths until the waves of nausea, one after another after another, subsided.

I clutched the handrail to avoid toppling down the steep brown steps, but I couldn't stop trembling, not even after I sat down.

There was a voice inside me, a whiny singsong voice. "Murder on Monday, murder on Friday, murder, murder," it repeated. And then I heard another voice, Eddie's, when he'd insisted on seeing me. "You're the one in the middle," he'd said.

"It isn't your fault, you know." I didn't know which voice that was until Mackenzie sat down next to me.

His voice was low and gentle, and he put his hand over mine. "You have nothing to do with what happened."

He was a decent man. I felt weak gratitude, and an overwhelming sense of shame and guilt. "I waited—I didn't call, didn't say, didn't tell you, and now he's—"

"It didn't just happen. It probably didn't happen within the last hour or two hours. He was burned, I think, but the coffee and the kettle are both cold. You couldn't have prevented it."

We sat on the steps silently waiting for the squad cars.

"It could be coincidence, too," Mackenzie said. "This could have nothing at all to do with Liza."

I would have liked to believe it.

The first man up the stairs paused. I stood up to unblock his path, and he eyed me with distaste. "Aren't you the one who...?" I was way past answering that one, but he took care of the problem himself. "Yeah, sure," he said. "I saw you in the papers. You're the one."

What was I supposed to say in return? That I didn't like finding corpses every few days?

"I'll wait outside," I told Mackenzie. He was already halfway back into the apartment. I needed sun and warmth.

But of course there wasn't any. I walked away from the chilly shadow of the building. Seated on the curb, my feet planted in the gutter, I tried to defrost in the diluted daylight.

What appeared to be dozens of men rushed up the stairs, carrying bags, stretchers, and God knows what. I knew some of what they'd do with their powders and measurements, and I wondered if the next tenant would be left, like me, to remove the residue of detection. Or was that the landlord's duty, and if so, why hadn't mine come to wash the walls? I knew my mind was floating, safely, I hoped, away from the building, away from the crowd of gapers gathering nearby.

"Sweetie, what's all this? Street's so noisy I couldn't hear my program. Sweetie!" She poked a finger in my shoulder. "What is this?"

She was fat and sloppy, her head wrapped in blue gauze over enormous pink rollers. She wore a bubble-gum-pink sweat suit and tennis shoes, sipped a can of diet soda, and looked ready to swallow me, the building, and any available gossip.

"I don't know. Please let me be."

"Well! Be that way!" She scuffed off, still sipping.

I looked back at the busy brown entrance to the apartment. The bakery downstairs, with its shiny empty trays, its small jolly placard, looked serenely out of place.

"What is it? What is it?" The man was near hysteria, and I swiveled around and peered through the crowd to identify him. He was short, elderly, and plump. Fear distorted the heavy features of his pink face. "What happened? Is Livvy here? She phoned. What's happening here?"

"That girl there knows," I heard the blue-headed lady say. "But she thinks she's too good to tell me."

He pushed through the crowd. I could see his feet in dark leather bedroom slippers approach, and then he was in front of me, waving his hands and shouting. "What happened, girlie? Tell me! It's my building. Livvy, this lady next door, she phoned me when she saw police."

He grunted and seated himself beside me. "My back," he said; then he put a scrubbed hand on my arm. "Please, girlie, please. What am I going to find up there? There's been a robbery?"

I couldn't think of an easy way to tell the truth, so I just told it. "A man died up there."

His face paled. "Gevalt! Eddie. It's Eddie? What is it, drugs? I knew something was up. Sophie said I should throw him out. *Dead?*" His tirade ended abruptly as if he'd suddenly, finally, heard what I'd said. "Dead?" he repeated, looking terrified.

I nodded.

"Must be drugs," he said after a lengthy pause. "I knew it Monday. Until then, he was pretty okay. But then, he was taking something. At 5:00 A.M., nobody laughs that way."

"What way?"

"He was crazy. Listen, he was never what you'd call normal, but he was normal crazy before Monday. I don't have an easy time finding assistants, with my hours. He's my assistant now a month, maybe longer. Comes in four, four-thirty, five, helps get the bread, the kaiser rolls, ready. Works till two, maybe three. With a break."

"But Monday? You said he—"

"I'm not a slave driver. He takes his coffee time; he's not exactly a fanatic worker anyway. And he likes the hours, he told me. An actor. Slept in the afternoons anyway. It's hard finding people."

"I'll bet. But what did you mean, crazy on Monday?"

"Crazy. What could crazy mean? Wild. High. Like on-drugs crazy. Crazy wife, too. Came in after he moved upstairs."

"Monday?"

"No, no. Before then. She screams at me. What did I do, she should scream at me? It's my fault that ganef doesn't support his own kids? I pay him. I told her to go to the police."

I tried once again. "Yes, but about Monday...?"

He buried his head in his hands. "I get one vacation a year. Pesach—Passover. You Jewish? You understand? No bread's allowed. The Exodus. No time for bread to rise leaving Egypt. Only unleavened bread. Matzo."

Theology and ritual law didn't seem pertinent, but I couldn't stop him.

"Can't use these ovens during those eight days. So once a year, I don't feel guilty closing shop, resting, sleeping when I want to. You don't know what it's like, girlie. I'm sitting, reading my paper, enjoying. Sophie's making chicken soup, you should only smell it. I didn't tell her about the phone call, thank God. She thinks I'm out for the air." He looked at me, tilting his head somewhat. He was small, despite his solid heaviness. "One vacation a year, you understand?" He looked down again.

"It must be rough," I said. He wasn't making the going exactly smooth for me, either, but I prompted one more time. "Monday? Crazy?"

"On Monday he's nuts. I told you already. Comes in. We're cleaning the ovens, getting ready to close them down. So on Monday he comes in a little meshuga. Says maybe he won't be back after Pesach. Maybe not ever. Won't need me or anybody or any job. Look, girlie, he's dancing around. Is that crazy or not? I was, between us, scared. Drugs, I figure to myself. Sophie says get him out of the apartment before he burns the place down. But I think about his wife, the little kiddies. And it's complicated. I pay him a little less, he gets the upstairs free. I'm not a rich man. It works for both of us. So how do I throw him out?"

He grunted again. "I have to go up there. Forty-six years in this country and no trouble. So now, when I'm an old man..." He sighed and waited, still afraid of what he'd face.

"About Monday. Did Eddie say why he might not come back?"

He shrugged. "Who understands from a crazy person? He says he's retiring. Maybe he got a Hollywood contract like he wanted." He scratched his scalp. It was pink and shiny, except for the thick fringe of white hair. "No, wait. He said something I didn't understand. It made him laugh crazier than ever when I asked. Sure, now I remember. I'm a baker. A baker here, a baker in the old country. So I don't understand everything American, even after forty-six years. Is that a crime? He should laugh at me that way?"

"About?"

"About my question, girlie. Like I said. You knew him?" He pulled back, suddenly aloof. "You are maybe the girl Livvy saw coming and going from the upstairs?"

"No."

"Yeah." He relaxed. "Livvy said the girl was little. Dark hair. Couldn't be you. You know, anyway, how he could laugh and make you feel like dirt? So I asked him what this loaf of mother was that he found. I know my bread, but this expression I never heard. I ask politely. And he laughs. A *load* of mother, he says. I still don't understand, so I repeat it. He drops his sponge like I made a big joke. Laughed and laughed. But mean. He was crazy."

"A load of mother?"

"That's it. What I said. Crazy, you see? High on something. Am I going to get it from Sophie."

I had an idea. "Could he have said 'mother lode'?" I asked.

"That's what I've been saying." He shook his head. "Oh, God. Dead." He struggled to get to his feet.

I stood up and helped him. He looked at me, his pink face near tears. He shook his head and glanced fearfully toward the brown doorway. "Crazy or not, the poor boy..." He wandered away without a farewell and stood near the upstairs entry, looking condemned. He went in.

What vein of gold had Eddie struck? I wondered. Monday, after Liza left. And why was he so ecstatic at dawn, and she was anything but?

"Hey, lady, look there," a freckled, gum-cracking teenager said. "You're a TV star."

A man on top of a car pointed a minicamera at me. I turned and galloped for the corner. I passed a bus sign. A little monitor in my brain clicked. This is where Liza must have waited, it said, marking the spot. If only the strike had started earlier, or Passover, if Liza hadn't needed to leave Eddie so early, if she hadn't been able to catch a bus from here to my house, then maybe...

But she was gone. And Eddie was gone. And as much as I sorrowed for them and felt horror at their fates, their lives had been very different from mine, and the more I found out about them, the less kinship I felt.

But what we had in common was enough, was the base common denominator: we had all been alive. The difference was, only I, the one in the middle, was still around.

Except, of course, for the murderer.

Eleven

MACKENZIE FOUND ME IN HIS CAR. "HOW DO you feel?" he asked, sliding in behind the wheel.

"No problem. Fine. I'm just fine." It somehow felt necessary, as a deputy, to play Brunhild the brave, to be professional about this, the way he was.

Mackenzie became very businesslike, carefully maneuvering the car into the swollen Friday-afternoon traffic.

"So, ah, tell me," I managed. "What did you guys decide up there?"

His voice was clinical. "Well, without tests to verify anything, he appears to have been burned on the face and hands and then bludgeoned. The back of his neck also looks burned as well as beaten. Burns were to stun him, most likely. First, with boiling water on the face. Hands burned trying to shield himself. Then with the kettle on the back of the neck. Maybe also a skillet that was in the sink. It had blood on it, apparently."

My stomach heaved.

We left the rows of neat red-brick houses, driving into and through a ragged wing of Fairmount Park.

Once I could no longer see the lines of stores and houses, I felt able to speak.

C.K. stared at the road, his eyes at their usual half-mast. We approached the shopping center at the SEPTA terminal. Mackenzie cut around corners, passed a few acres of slumbering buses, and placed us smack in the center of a traffic jam. "Damn strike," he said.

Horns honked furiously and futilely all around us. "Come on, Mandy," he said. "Give me something to listen to besides these horns and this nonmusic and my own escalatin' blood pressure. Talk about what's upset-tin' you."

"I can't. All I want to do is avoid it, get past it. I have a better idea if you're suddenly in the mood for self-revelation. How about if you stop hiding behind your initials?"

He looked at me as if I were mildly amusing, then paid attention to the traffic jam again. Two cars in one of the converging lanes managed to get through a light. We inched forward and waited again.

"I don't care about your name. Not really. But is it Claude? I would understand avoiding Claude."

"No, and it isn't Rumpelstiltskin, either. Why don't you think of C.K. as a name? Kind of Indian-sound-ing, isn't it? Seekay. Why does it concern you so much?"

"Why do my private thoughts and fears concern you so much?"

"Because—"

"And aren't they obvious, anyway? I'm the one in the *middle*. That's what Eddie said to me. Now I under-stand. Liza saw Eddie, then Liza saw me. Then Liza got killed. Then Eddie saw me. Then Eddie got killed. I'm left, and I'm scared. It doesn't matter if I know anything. Somebody thinks I do. Somebody thought Eddie did. Somebody was searching for something in that apartment, and I don't know what it was or if they found it. I hope like hell they did, that accounts are settled. But I can't believe in it. And anybody who's already killed twice, to amend your theory, won't quibble about a third murder, will he? I'm scared, Mackenzie. I'm really scared."

"Of course you are. You're gutsy, but not so oblivious as to be insane. We have a real problem here."

We. The little word blanketed and coddled me. I no longer felt like a target, alone on an enormous field. Mackenzie smiled and nodded.

"Keeping you safe's my job and my preference," he said quietly.

As he spoke, we made it through the intersection at last, and I felt released from a terrible pressure. I also felt that the two of us had just passed a personal landmark, and a covenant had been made, a promise between us. I was now pulsing and trembling from a schizy mix of anxiety and pleasurable anticipation of my dual-purpose escort.

We drove into the city, past rows of boarded-up stores, Laundromats, bars, and discount shoe shops. Mackenzie did a smooth slalom around the iron supports of the elevated lines on Market Street.

"I'm exhausted," I said. I had relaxed all the way into near coma.

"Can you hold up awhile longer? I have to make a stop and then, well, I owe you a night on the town, don't I? Didn't we have a delayed date? For your mother's sake? How about dinner?" He finally looked over at me and opened his overlarge smile that erased the sleepy hayseed and replaced it with—I don't know what. Something more intriguing.

I smiled and settled back, feeling infinitely better. I

would have personal police protection for a while
longer. Besides, his expression had reminded me that
no matter what was true of the bodies I'd found, mine
was still in working order.

We turned left and were back in the neighborhood of
old homes fronted with wide porches. He stopped in
front of the one with the broken green railing. "Stick
around," he said casually.

I wasn't sure if he meant I should stay alive or hang
on to his jacket. I chose to do both. I opened the car
door to accompany him.

He looked surprised, so he'd obviously been speaking metaphorically, but I wasn't into figures of speech
just then, and I wasn't into being alone. "It won't be
pleasant," he said. "No matter how she felt about him.
It's never easy."

It wasn't. First, she eyed us through a half-open
door. "He's no good," she said. A television blared
away inside. "I don't care what trouble he's in. I have
enough trouble from him already."

"It isn't about that, ma'am. Not that way." Somehow,
Mackenzie had the ability to be heard over *Sesame Street*,
even while murmuring.

She let us in. Really, she let him in, eyeing me with
overt hostility.

Mackenzie took her into the kitchen, and I eased into
an overstuffed chair near the TV. "A-B-C-D-D-D-" the
set shouted. The kids were mesmerized, which was just
as well. They didn't hear Catherine Bayer cry out and
moan. They didn't look up when she walked back into
the room. She started toward them, then turned and
sank onto a worn sofa, a slab of foam on what looked
like a door with legs. She shook her head in a silent no.

"I never thought," she said, still shaking. "I mean,
trouble, yes, but I didn't mean that kind of trouble.

Not to be...murdered? His head? You said they hurt his head?"

When Mackenzie nodded, she broke into sobs, muffling them into the hard wedge that backed the couch. "I don't know why I carry on like this," she said, wiping her nose with her hand. I offered her a pack of tissues, and she took it without looking at me. She blew her nose loudly. The children stared at the set.

"His face," she said, and she sighed deeply. The head shaking never stopped. "It was the whole problem. The reason for all his troubles. He was so good-looking. Women liked him."

I hoped Mackenzie wouldn't speed up her grief so that he could ask questions. He didn't. He pulled a chipped chair out from the dining room and straddled it. I had a vision of him sitting in an endless succession of chairs, their backs shields against an ongoing chorus of crying women.

"Why?" the woman asked. "Why now? He was so excited about the future. Why now?"

"What was he excited about?" Mackenzie spoke casually.

She shrugged. "I don't know. See, he didn't pay support. We aren't legally separated. No papers or anything." She began the head shaking again and seemed absorbed in her own thoughts.

"But something happened recently?" Mackenzie prompted.

She shrugged. "I don't know what it was. But see, I had gone to the shop, the bakery, to complain. I can't get a job. I don't know anything to do that pays more than getting somebody to watch the kids costs. I needed money. So I went there with the kids last weekend. It wasn't the first time. Ed said he didn't have anything to give me. I got angry. How am I supposed to live? I said I was calling the cops. He practically threw me out, said his boss would fire him if I made scenes, and then where would we be?"

She paused, sighed, pleated the fabric of her blouse, and took a while to relive the ugly scene. "But Monday," she continued, "Monday afternoon he came here and said everything was going to be different. He gave me a hundred dollars his boss had given him. He said it was only the beginning. That there would be a lot more."

"Did he say where he was going to get the money?" Mackenzie kept his voice low and distant, like someone who was only casually interested. I wondered if the baker had told him about the mother lode and Eddie's manic mood.

Mrs. Bayer shook her head even more vigorously. "We fought about it. I was sure it was from something wrong, that something would go wrong with it. It always does. He's had horses, movie contracts, deals. Always something. But, at least, those times he'd tell me what it was. Monday he wouldn't say where it would come from, only that it would be a lot. So I knew it was something really wrong."

She pulled the edges of her exhausted tissue, then bunched it up and pushed it into her pocket. "So," she said, "we had another fight and I kicked him out. Told him to go to his girl. There was always a girl. Let her put up with him, not me. And I never saw him again. Not even Wednesday, his birthday. We had a cake for him. He said he'd be by."

I knew where he'd been Wednesday. That was the night I visited the Playhouse. I remembered Eddie's friend, the man who'd talked about a party, about how Eddie stayed so young. And Eddie had invited me, a complete stranger, to join that birthday party, while his children and wife waited here with their cake.

Sesame Street wound down. "I'm hungry," the little boy said. "What's dinner?"

Either they had gone blind watching TV, or the sight of their mother crying was familiar enough to make no impression. "Maaaaa, what can I eat?" Doreen, product but not inheritor of Eddie's good looks, was a whiner.

Catherine Bayer stared at her children as if they were extraterrestrials. Then she turned her head this way and that, back and forth from Mackenzie to me. "What am I going to do?" she asked, her voice hollow.

"Mom?" the little boy asked.

She gave a wrenching sigh. "I don't know anything more." She rose and walked to the door, opening it as if it were made of lead. "I have to start taking care of things," she added dully.

We drove through the thick dusk silently. The morning, this exciting morning, when I'd "solved" the mystery, realized who the bear was, had happened to somebody else, in prehistoric times. Even the air was exhausted. The sky had collapsed and was lying soggily on the hood of the car. I felt worn and soiled.

"Mackenzie, is that dinner date for real?"

He nodded. He was not a master of small talk, but he was my protector, and that made up for a lot.

"Okay, then. But first I'd like to pick up my car, go home, shower, and have a drink before dinner. And I'd like you to join me. In the house and the drink. Not the shower."

For once, he followed directions.

* * *

Maybe it was immoral in the light of the day's events, but with Mackenzie guarding my hearth downstairs and a fast, hot spray pelting me upstairs, I began to feel like one of those singing soap ads. I slathered suds hither and yon, checking for missing parts. I was still all there.

I put on fresh makeup, perfume, and a peach silk blouse that makes my skin look dewy and my hair burnished. I left the two top buttons open. I chose a soft woolen skirt that swings niftily when I move and went downstairs to rejoin the resident detective.

"You're a miracle of regeneration," he said. He had already poured himself a glass of wine and he was reclining, somewhat possessively, in the room he'd analyzed so offensively. But that had been a very long time ago.

I got the jug of wine out of the refrigerator and poured myself a glass and settled beside him. I looked longingly at the empty pottery ashtray on the coffee table. It was close to the perfect moment for a lazy smoke, but there wasn't even a two-puff stub around to cheat with.

Mackenzie was not into the spirit of things. At least not into my interpretation. He seemed coiled and tense. He swirled the wine around and stared at it, forgetting to make a caustic remark about its vintage; then he sipped with an abstracted air. Maybe I should have rushed things more and invited him to share my shower, too.

I sighed and lounged, and he responded by gazing at my ceiling. I sighed again. He looked at his watch. "You mind?" he mumbled, all the while heaving himself up and flicking on the television.

"Negotiations continue on the transit strike, and a

spokesman for the drivers said a settlement is possible if management will agree to..."

I didn't want to hear about the strike, about traffic choking the Schuylkill Expressway, or about what Mackenzie was waiting for. "Why play it all over again?" I asked, but he shrugged and kept on staring.

"...body of thirty-year-old actor Eddie Bayer found in his Overbrook Park apartment this afternoon, an apparent homicide victim. No leads have been..." I poured more wine. "The Philadelphia Playhouse announces cancellation of this evening's performance. All tickets will be refunded."

I remembered the minicamera, and like Mackenzie, I, too, focused on the set. The camera panned the crowd outside the building. And then it paused on an impossibly haggard me, deep in conversation with the little baker.

"Well, at least they didn't give my name," I said.

"I asked them not to." Mackenzie clicked off the set and returned to his silent meditations. This was not the evening I had primed for upstairs. My favorite blouse, my most expensive perfume, were going to waste. Four seconds before I was going to call the paramedics to resuscitate him, Mackenzie shifted position on the sofa.

"Hey," I said forcefully, remembering a topic that was sure to annoy him into attention, "I've got it, you're Chester, right? So here's to you, Chester K. Mackenzie, the life of the party."

He was my least alert gentleman caller since drunk Richard Whitney passed out on my mother's shag rug in eleventh grade. This one stared at me, then yawned very intently. "It isn't Chester," he said finally.

He scratched his ear, where an errant curl must have been tickling him, and looked at me with distant curiosity. I wondered how the man could send out such clear and sensual signals, and then just lose it altogether. Or had I made up a subtext to what he had been saying.

I didn't feel clever or creative enough to figure out where we had wandered or how to bring us back. I began to slump in unconscious imitation of Mackenzie. I watched him ruminate. From time to time, his coma was interrupted as he studied his notebook.

"Come on, Mackenzie," I finally said, "can't you stop detecting for a while? Aren't you burned out? It's time for dinner." Surely he hadn't lost that appetite, too. "Time for being people," I added. "Want to try it? Or anything?" The last sort of popped out.

He stood up, unwinding himself until he was his full, slouchy height. He allowed a hint of his great white smile. "Sorry. I can't seem to get off it yet. I'll try. I'll try." He went into the kitchen area and poured himself a second glass of wine. One of the many small acts that had erased the D.J. from my life was his instant paralysis when he required sustenance. "Oh, boy," he'd say, "could I go for a cup of coffee." But he never did. What he meant was "Could I wait for a cup of coffee. You go." Now Mackenzie was definitely less verbal than the disc jockey, but he wasn't into precious helplessness, and if you're single long enough, you learn to cherish small miracles.

Just as we were beginning something resembling human interaction, the phone rang. I sometimes wish I'd lived out my days before that smart-ass Bell let everybody intrude on everybody else at whim.

Mackenzie lifted the receiver. "Hello?" he said. Then he held it out for me. "It's for you." He seemed surprised.

I glanced at the clock. Six forty-five. Cheap-call time, and good old guess-who was taking advantage of

economy pestering time. It was not her habit to call
more than once a week, but then it was not my habit to
stumble over corpses often, either, so I couldn't be-
grudge her concern. Only her timing.

"Hello, Mother." I waited. A man had answered,
after all.

"My...date, Mom. We're getting ready to leave for
dinner. Yes, the same one. Mackenzie. That's his last
name. His first name is...Chuck."

Mackenzie sprang to attention. "Chuck!" he said
with so much incredulity and annoyance I was sure I
had hit it. "Chuck!"

My mother decided that Chuck was an acceptable
first name in her book. Obviously, all was well with
me. I had a date with a man with a first and last name.

I watched Mackenzie take out his ratty notebook
again, still trying to make his scribbles merge into a
coherent whole. For the moment, my mother was
more interesting than he was.

"What's the matter with Herman?" I asked, inter-
rupting a long, solemn windup. "He's bald? Mom,
that's the funniest—"

I pulled the receiver away from my ear to deflect a
short series of indignant screeches. "Mother," I finally
said, "I do not consider him my little brother."

Mackenzie looked up from his notebook.

"Let Daddy and Herman work it out, then. But if
the doctor said...okay, then skip ball games. Let him
watch soap operas."

Mackenzie closed his notebook.

"Mom, Chuckie's waiting for me." Magic words. She
paused, weighing Chuck against bald Herman.
"Mother, dear," I said to speed things to a conclusion,
"it's not fair to make Herman live in the bathroom. No
wonder he's depressed."

Mackenzie's eyes were no longer droopy.

Mother gave up. She was stranded a thousand miles to the south, left to deal with her tragedy alone.

Mackenzie looked at me with new interest as I returned to his side. "I give up," he said. "Talk about skeletons in the closet. Your brother lives in a bathroom?"

He was alert, alive. Cute. Emitting those rays again. My mother had saved the day. "I'll explain, Mackenzie, if you swear you'll retire from detecting for a while."

"I'll consider it."

"And first, you'll have to understand that the woman on the phone cannot conceivably be my true genetic mother. She is an eccentric who picked me out from Rent-A-Child, and that entitles her to unlimited phone calls once the rates are down."

"And Herman? He's no relation, either?"

"Are you ready, Clyde?" He didn't even flinch. What the hell did that *C* stand for? "Herman is my mother's parrot."

"She called him your little brother?"

"She can't figure out how to make me feel involved in his destiny, guilty about his mental health and happiness, but she tries. Constantly. At one point, she tried insisting that he was an endangered species, but that didn't do it. Now he's my sibling."

"Hold it—Herman's a bald parrot?" He laughed.

"Yes. He's pulled out all his lovely green feathers."

"God, but that's sad," he said.

"They have been to the best doctor in Miami. A specialist, no less. After all, we have not only a nude parrot, but a messy, feathery bathroom floor."

"Ah, yes. And why does he live in the bathroom?"

"Because my father hates him, and it's a small apartment. He started out in the living room, but he drove Dad insane."

Mackenzie sat back, his arms folded, a wide smile on his face, and I no longer questioned my attraction for him.

"The bedroom was out," I continued, "and a windowless closet seemed cruel and unusual punishment. My father claims to be constipated since the bird-in-the-bathroom evolved, but he tries to cope."

Mackenzie grinned. He looked relaxed and vulnerable. I am not a nice person. I took advantage of it.

"Clarence?" I whispered.

"You'll never guess," he said lazily, "so continue."

"Well, C—may I call you C? Or is that presumptuous? The specialist told Mother that the bird was bored. Waiting to hear the next toilet flush isn't enough to keep a parrot perky. Pulling out feathers was a way to fill the time."

"What's to become of him?"

His arms were stretched out on the back pillows of the sofa, his fingers only inches from my shoulder. I could feel his body heat, or force field, while I spoke. "The doctor suggested TV. Sports are out because Daddy will not have a squawking bird share his games. So, either the rummy-tile ladies are going to know that Mama's got a naked bird behind the shower curtain, or she has to figure out what kind of programming appeals to parrots."

Mackenzie closed his eyes and smiled. "Goddamn," he said, and laughed out loud. Then he sat up. "Mind if I make myself comfortable?" he asked.

Frankly, I was delighted. He put his notebook on the coffee table and took off his camel-colored jacket.

Then he stretched, and I could see his ribs press against the fine blue fabric of his shirt.

He turned and looked at me. Really looked at me. His eyes, his face, his mass of silvered hair were hushed and waiting and very beautiful.

But I couldn't stop looking at his blue shirt. Or rather at the gun that nestled beneath his arm. I felt as if he had taken off a mask and become somebody I wasn't sure I wanted to meet. Or else, I had taken off blinders and found who he really was. "Put it away, please," I said. "Somewhere I can't see it."

He nodded sadly. "I think you're fine, Amanda Pepper," he said softly, but there was a wistful tone in his voice that frightened me. He carefully undid the leather contraption on his chest and put it and its contents on the floor, out of sight. "But I don't think we can make it."

"Why?" I whispered.

"Because of that. Because of who I am, what I do. Because of how it's been. What's happened. How we met." He kept looking at me. "My timing's off, my sense of where to go, how to proceed. My job keeps overlappin' onto what should be us, and I can't seem to stop it. An' I don' want to mess up somethin' that could be... real fahn."

His drawl increased with his hesitancy.

I was moved by his confusion, his sensitivity. I didn't have to look at the gun on the floor, and I didn't want to consider our past, the scenes behind us. I wanted to erase the taste of death the only way that seemed possible. But I couldn't say that, wouldn't literally drag corpses back into our world right now. So I took both his hands in mine. They were good hands, human hands, strong hands. Without the gun, he was a man, and a fine one.

"Forget your job," I said softly. "This is after-hours. A separate story altogether. It's like curling up with a good book. Your character's been established, and so has mine. A strong mutual interest has been clearly demonstrated, some interesting complications, and—"

"You're not forgettin' your job, English teacher."

"Shh. Anyway, it's relevant. We're at the end of the introduction, Mackenzie. The end of the beginning. Now we have to get to the denouement, the unraveling of the mystery. Our mystery."

He grinned. "You sure?" he asked, and I nodded. I could see his wide shoulders relax, could feel the muscles of his hands uncoil as I held them. "You are one fahn instructor," he said, and I was suddenly, finally, being held, enveloped by him. "It's just that I do believe—" he said, and he kissed me, and it was the way I had hoped the curl of his lips would feel. "I do believe," he said again after a long while, cupping my face in his hands, "that where I come from—" and he lifted my hair and kissed the nape of my neck, my ears, my temples—"mah English teachers told me that in dramatic structure—" and he pulled me closer still and we held each other, rocking quietly—"before the denouement, there is another significant step—" and his hand behind me stroked my back, sliding slowly down the silk—"known as the climax, I do believe."

"I do believe so myself," I said, and then we didn't say much for a long time. There was too much to find out.

There was Mackenzie and his gold-toned skin to explore; there was the way he turned his slow Southern tempo into a lazy, timeless voluptuousness. And with him, through him, I felt just as new, redefined and given shape in the endless moment we shared.

All I can say is that the man knows his dramatic structure.

"You're very beautiful," he whispered eventually. "An extraordinary woman. Very fine."

"Your drawl is gone."

"It's a symptom of stress," he said. "It is also a fahn aphrodisiac for Yankee women. Almost as effective as your leavin' the top two buttons open on that silky, touchy thing you were wearin'."

"Mackenzie, you are one smug, supercilious Southerner. And very fahn as well."

"And a man of honor. I promised you dinner, didn't I?"

"Miss Peppah?" he said when we were reassembled and ready to leave, "it has been an honor and a privilege to make your acquaintance."

I curtsied. I came damn near to simpering.

We didn't have any sunset to walk off into. But then, we weren't playing for an audience.

Twelve

DINNER AT EIGHT IS MUCH MORE CIVILIZED, anyway, and I was starving.

We walked toward Walnut Street, pausing in front of various eating options.

"Too crowded," he said at the first.

"No...not in the mood for Chinese," I said at the second.

"You sure?" he asked. "You know, all the Chinese restaurateurs' children are off studying computer science, so in a few years you'll have to order software, not mushi pork."

"Too ferny," he said at our next opportunity.

"Just right!" I finally declared when we found ourselves outside the inexpensive Italian place where Gus and I had eaten a few nights earlier. "No atmosphere. Just old Christmas cards pasted all over the walls, if that intrigues you. But great food and lots of it."

They had cannelloni stuffed with liver. I no longer admit my liver fixation until I know someone very well and trust him. I had once dated—once—the most incredible pompous ass it has been my misfortune to know. He had a lineage that would bring half the city to its knees, and he hadn't done poorly himself. He was a snob about his ancestors, his schools, his seats at the Philadelphia Orchestra, and worst of all, about food. And when I ordered liver instead of the currently chic entrée, he was as upset as if I'd demanded peanut butter and jelly on white bread.

It was okay with Mackenzie. He didn't even flinch.

He studied the cards on the wall. I, meanwhile, having not smoked afterward for the first time, sublimated an acute desire for a cigarette by attacking the breadsticks in the basket. I wondered whether full lungs or full hips were less acceptable.

"Listen to this," Mackenzie said. "'Maybe a reindeer will find its way, And bring you joy and mirth today.' Or, 'This wish is sincere, it is the truest. May your New Year be the newest.'"

I wasn't in a literary mood, so while he scanned the verses, I scanned the room. Men don't seem to have the same driving need to examine and assess every passerby while eating. Or at least my men defer to my fierce lunge for the seat with a view. They also seem less able to eavesdrop on neighboring tables while conducting a conversation. Their restaurant experiences are poor, dim, one-dimensional events.

Anyway, Mackenzie was feeding his soul with the waste products of the Muse, so he didn't notice when in walked one Augustus Winston III. It was easy to miss Gus, even if one was watching the door. He looked diminished, grayed out, and pulpy instead of lined. He nodded to the owner and limped toward a small table near the rear.

He seemed in need of a friend. I mentally squirmed. If you've had your sense of guilt as carefully nurtured as I have, there are certain no-win situations.

One of them is when you have to choose between a new sex object and an old friend. I sighed. "Gus is over there," I said.

"Invite him over," Mackenzie said.

He was a marvel, accepting first my liver, then my friend. I was hopeful, too, that a leisurely meal and some wine would smooth away the edge of suspicion between the two men. It took a while to catch Gus's eye, but I did, and gestured extravagantly for him to join us. He limped over, eyeing Mackenzie with suspicion before seating himself.

"I, ah, there's no show tonight," he said by way of introduction and explanation. "You heard about Eddie Bayer?" Obviously, Gus wasn't a fan of the six o'clock news. "What's going on? Liza, now Eddie. Is somebody killing off our whole troupe?"

It was a new angle. "Do you think it's the ghost of an outraged playwright?" I picked at the crumbs of my breadstick.

Nobody even smiled. I realized that my little summit meeting was probably not a terrific idea.

"How did you hear about Eddie?" Mackenzie asked Gus.

There went the evening. It had been fun and games for a while. Oh, much more than that. But we were back on the black brick road, stomping on down to the slough of despond. I experienced my first case of postcoital depression.

When Gus finally answered Mackenzie, he sounded cautious and verbose at the same time. Very unlike himself.

"Cathy called. His wife. She needed to talk to somebody, anybody, I guess. Needed to say what had happened, over and over again. Called herself a widow woman, said she had to start handling things, taking charge of her life, but she was scared. Didn't know how. She babbled about life insurance and day-care centers and retraining programs and didn't make lots of sense. I tried to calm her, to slow her down, but she went on and on about the list of things she had to do by herself."

I said a silent prayer for poor Catherine Bayer. May she get a belated handle on her life.

"And she talked about women," Gus continued. "Eddie's women. One who'd caused trouble, and even about a police woman who'd come looking for him. A tall woman with...and her partner, a cop from the South, and..."

I snapped another breadstick into four segments and proceeded to eat one at a time.

"You, Mandy?" Gus said. "It wasn't you, was it? Did you...Eddie, too?"

I nodded.

"What's with you? Why would you be there?" He stopped talking as if somebody had corked up his mouth. His lined face looked like a turtle's pulling into its shell.

I shrugged, trying to imitate James Bond's attitude toward danger and death. That is, of course, James Bond stuffing his mouth with breadsticks. "I was in the wrong place at the wrong time," I said. "I was supposed to—" But Mackenzie was shaking his head no in slow motion, boring into me with an icy blue-eyed silencer, and I stopped. Cleverly, I simply ate more, carbo loading for some unknown marathon ahead.

Surely Gus wasn't under suspicion again, or still? The Pooh business had cleared him, hadn't it? He wasn't the Winnie. But then, the gold charm had been for Eddie, and he wasn't "it," either. The gold charm had ultimately meant nothing. I peered at Gus from behind a new wall of reserve. The lines on his face had become crevasses.

Nobody spoke. It could have gone on that way throughout eternity had not Giorgio, the waiter, found Gus in his new spot. "Ah, Mr. Winston, a night of surprises! First you are here late, and then you go and confuse me with the musical chairs." Luckily, Giorgio was fond of solos, because he waved the air with his oversize menu and continued despite the lack of response from our trio of zombies. "No matter, no matter!" he practically sang. "What can Giorgio bring you tonight? The calamari is—" Since the language had no words excellent enough for the squid, Giorgio brought his hand to his mouth and kissed it, loudly. "And the stuffed ziti—what can I say? Maria's grandmother's recipe. Old country. Perfect. Our eggplant? The house sauce is—"

"Spaghetti, Giorgio," Gus said. "Meat sauce."

"Spaghetti? Spaghetti? What kind of choice is spaghetti with meat sauce? For that you can go to the supermarket."

"Spaghetti, Giorgio," Gus repeated, and the waiter departed with a histrionic sigh.

Gus leaned over the table. "Now listen, Mack—"

"Mackenzie," C.K. said, and his voice was like a slap.

Gus's skin took on a mauve tinge. "Mackenzie, then. You'd better—"

"Ah! You make Giorgio so surprised he forgot to ask about the wine!" The waiter had regained his sunny Mediterranean zest, and he stood on tiptoe, waiting for the thrill of Gus's wine choice.

"Red."

"Red? You are sick, perhaps, tonight? Red, like a crayon? I have a Bardolino; it will make you happy again. It will make your heart sing. It is for men."

Giorgio flexed his muscles like a strong man; then he hugged himself. "But tender, too. Or a Chianti Classico that—"

"Fine," Gus said. "That's fine."

Giorgio backed off like a whipped dog. But luckily, at the next table, four buxom women in flowery dresses waited with anxious delight for something to spark their evening. Giorgio put in Gus's wine order, reinflated himself, and danced over to them.

During which performance, our table maintained its funereal silence.

"You were about to say something?" Mackenzie prompted. "Something vaguely threatening?"

Gus's shoulders drooped. "Not threatening. But dammit, Mackenzie, why involve her in this? You don't need a date to hunt corpses. Leave her out of it."

"I'll assume you mean that as her friend, Winston. So as her friend—which I am as well—stop butting in. Stop giving advice. She's okay. I'm not involving her in anything."

I was obviously not there. I must have left and not noticed it, the way they were discussing me. "Hi!" I said brightly. "Maybe you'd be interested in hearing how I am from me?" Nobody noticed, so I retreated and watched them volley. I pretended it was Wimbledon.

"Well, you're sure botching it if you're not trying to involve her," Gus snapped. "She's around two dead bodies in one week. That's some track record. Are you badgering her about this one, too?"

"Did it appear to you that I brought Miss Peppah here to badger her?" Mackenzie drawled. "And anyway, why would I? Do you see some connection between the deaths? Other than your brilliant theory that somebody's stalking your ensemble."

My cannelloni was slipped in front of me with the grace of a matador's pass. "And you!" Giorgio said to Mackenzie with a chuckle. "Osso buco for the gentleman." He lowered his voice to a mournful lament. "And spaghetti with meat sauce for Mr. Winston." He filled our glasses.

"There was talk about Eddie and Liza," Gus said, looking at his wine. "But there was always talk about both of them separately, too. So who knows?"

"Or maybe nobody would gossip specifically about Liza in front of you," Mackenzie said. "Possible?"

Gus looked in danger of disintegrating into the spaghetti strands. "Maybe," he acknowledged.

"But still," I told the tablecloth. "Even so..." The men watched each other.

"And what would that talk have to do with murders?" Gus had worked his face back to something like its normal sandpaper contours. He drew lines in his congealing meat sauce with his fork.

"The food's getting cold," I said, eating some of mine. My cannelloni responded warmly, but nothing else did.

"Maybe the talk means nothing. Maybe everything. You know what does mean something?" Mackenzie pointed his fork at Gus. "Liza," he said forcibly. "Liza."

Both times he said the name, Gus recoiled, as if the fork, or something, pierced him.

"Liza is where it started," Mackenzie continued. "Eddie's death is connected because he was connected to Liza."

"I still don't know what you mean, ultimately," Gus said stiffly.

"I don't know about ultimates, Winston. But it means, to me, that he died because he knew who killed

Liza Nichols. He knew something incriminatin' that
the killer couldn't risk having exposed. Or, at the very
least, the killer *thought* he knew something."

There was somebody else in town who might be
thought to know something And I liked her very
much. I didn't like going through another round of
reasons why I was prime target number three.

Gus pronounced each word distinctly as if tutoring a
rather slow learner. "And do you have any idea who
this person is who wanted to kill Liza? And do you
have any idea why?"

"Maybe," Mackenzie said. "But that is, after all, literally my business. And while we're on the subject,
where were you this morning before the funeral?"

Gus's face became splotched. "Dammit, are you suggesting—"

"The food is cold," I said. "I thought we came here
for dinner."

They looked at me as if I'd just bopped in off the
street and tried to sell them my mother's body for a few
bucks.

"Mandy," Gus said after he recognized me, "I still
don't understand your role in all this." He turned back
to C.K. "And you never answered me. Leave her out
of this. It's dangerous. For God's sake, you know that.
If she keeps hanging around the scenes of murders, if
she keeps looking like an auxiliary policeman, then
she's liable to get hurt."

Mackenzie looked more likely to devour Gus than
the osso buco.

"Listen to me!" I was so loud that the four flowers at
the next table stopped talking and looked over. I lowered my voice. "I'm here. I'm sick of being discussed
and debated while I'm right here. You're scaring me
and ruining dinner. Shut up and eat!"

They listened to me. Giorgio, however, was not going to be pleased by the pushed-around messes left on Gus's and my plates. Mackenzie alone managed to eat.

"I, ah, have to go," Gus said after he'd disfigured his spaghetti. "Meeting at the Playhouse, even if there's no show." He gave a small, unhappy chuckle. "We're having some casting difficulties. Losing people. I'll excuse myself, if you don't mind." He pulled out his wallet and stood up.

"Gus." I reached out and touched his hand. "I didn't mean to sound harsh. I know you care and you're trying to protect me. But I'll be okay. I promise not to find any more corpses."

"I don't want to find yours," he grumbled; then he limped away to the cashier.

"You didn't have to lay into him that way," I told Mackenzie. "He was trying to be kind."

"You sure?" Mackenzie's voice wasn't precisely a lover's caress. "You sure he wasn't upset because somebody he likes may become so involved in this that he has to get rid of her, too?"

"That's disgusting. That's perverted. You've got tunnel vision, some hang-up about your role in life. You see everybody and everything as suspicious. Gus isn't—"

"Cleared. Gus isn't cleared. Drop back a few mental steps and consider. He still has no alibi for Monday, and God knows about this morning. He's a man who knows how to hate, and no matter how warped, he had a reason to hate Liza. You know, hell hath no fury like a woman scorned—except for the amazin' fury of some scorned men. And finally, Miss Peppah, you do not have access to all the available information anyway."

"Such as?"

"You want dessert?"

I sighed and shook my head.

"Good." He surprised me by helping me with my chair.

It was drizzling in a pleasant, soft way. A fine, almost invisible spray coated my skin by the time we got home.

My house looked warm and inviting, a stage for fantasies we could wrap around us. I still had firewood left from the winter, and a bottle of brandy somewhere, and . . .

"Winston was right about one thing," Mackenzie said. "You can't keep on being seen with me. Some nut's going to think you know what's going on. Not that you do, of course."

"Not if you keep being evasive and cryptic and asking me about dessert when you could give me hard facts. But that's okay with me. Let's stay invisible. We'll hide in here."

"That wasn't what I—"

I kissed him lightly. "Excuse me for a minute?" Upstairs, I readied my bed and bod for the great Pepper-Mackenzie reunion I had penciled in for the remainder of the night.

"Good idea," Mackenzie said when I was back downstairs.

"You read minds, too?"

"I'll be a minute," he said, heading for the staircase himself. "Wait here."

He didn't read minds. What he did was take the stairs two at a time.

"Hey there," he shouted down after a few minutes.

I knew he'd catch on eventually. I walked to the stairs and was on the first tread before he called out again.

"Mind if I use this phone? I have to make a call. Business."

I sat down on the staircase, refusing to be discouraged. I didn't like his working hours, his compartmentalized mind, or the fact that I was so obviously shut out of this particular compartment that he was hiding in the bedroom to make a call. I moved up two steps and listened.

He sounded tired. "I was tied up around seven, Ray. Couldn't call."

I remembered the tie-up fondly. And remembering, I moved up two more treads.

"Tense as hell. He overexplained how he heard about it. Check whether Catherine Bayer really called him."

I could picture him standing by my bed, foolishly ignoring it.

"I think I've got someone up there who'll loosen up about the records. Tomorrow, I expect."

That made no sense. I moved up another step.

"Everybody. All of them. Between nine and twelve this morning. We'll go over it later."

He sounded finished. I crept down the stairs, afraid to be caught eavesdropping. I realized that the little pile of mail I'd picked up this afternoon was still on the coffee table. It looked like an uninspired collection of bills and sale announcements. Mackenzie's voice became loud and annoyed. I could hear him clearly from where I sat in the living room. "Yeah, well I'm workin' the same hours, Raymond, so we're both doin' slave labor."

More silence. I arranged myself seductively on the sofa, checked out my phone bill, and then realized that the last envelope had nothing on it. No address, no return address, no stamp. It had been shoved through the mail slot.

"Amnesty International would not be interested!" Mackenzie boomed into the phone upstairs.

I could not have explained the ominous sense that white envelope produced except that it was not the way an envelope should look. It had not arrived the way mail is supposed to. Obviously, my tolerance for the unexpected had dropped to zero. I cautiously ripped it open.

Mackenzie loped down the stairs. "That Raymond never quits," he said. "As if I weren't workin', too. As if—"

His voice seemed very distant. I was completely engrossed in unfolding my mail in slow motion. Mackenzie came over and sat next to me just in time to see the most primitive, least-welcome message I'd ever received.

It wasn't verbose. There were only three words, all cut from what appeared newspaper headlines and ads, then taped onto the page. Even so, it made its point. Eloquently. All it said was:

1. ~~HER~~
2. ~~HIM~~
3. YOU

"HER" and "HIM" were crossed out, items taken care of on a list of things to do today. I looked at the "YOU" until the letters seemed to levitate and come closer to meet me. Until Mackenzie gently removed the paper from my shaking hand.

Thirteen

I FELT LIKE A KID BEING SHUTTLED OFF TO camp, only I didn't have name tags in my neckband.

We progressed in silence until Mackenzie again insisted that much as he would have liked to, he couldn't stay with me, that he had to work.

I suggested that he would show adequate interest in me only when I, too, became a corpse.

He suggested that I had a tendency toward the irrational, that I'd be safe in the suburbs, that the murderer was a childish coward.

I said something unprintable.

He said an English teacher should use the language more creatively.

I didn't say anything. The reference to my profession shocked me. It doesn't take much to distract me: a couple of murders, a new lover, a direct threat to my life, and zap—pedagogical duties slip my mind. I slumped down as much as the seat belt would allow. "Damn. I'm giving a test Monday, and I didn't bring my notes."

"Good. Your mind will be creatively occupied, then."

We drove slowly enough. Mackenzie didn't seem in any fierce rush to get on with his policing. He avoided the Expressway, even though there was a chance of its moving smoothly at this hour. We made our way toward Beth's safe harbor, passing T.G.I.F. celebrants on both Penn's and Drexel's campuses, past unreclaimed turf with hopeless, abandoned houses, past the zoo. A camel, peering over the fence at us, chewed sideways, looking as bored as I expected to be.

This was not my idea of how to spend a weekend. I'm not ever fond of deferring gratification, and with a death-threat, it seems an even sillier way to spend the remaining time.

We finally reached Beth's share of prime Main Line real estate. "Nice house," Mackenzie said. "Nice goin'." He turned off the motor. "Okay, do you have it straight?"

I nodded. It wasn't hard to learn. "I shalt not leave the bosom of my family."

"I believe it's 'shall' in the first person. But the most important commandment is: Thou shalt not indulge in the urge to sleuth."

"My, but those words trip right off your tongue. You have a pathological delusion about your godlike self, don't you? Now I know what that *C* stands for. No wonder you didn't want to reveal your true identity. But even He had a first name."

"Listen, Mandy, I've grown fond of your body. I'd like it to stay intact. So relax and enjoy spring in the country."

I lapsed into sulking. From necessity, not chivalry, he opened my car door and took me gently by the arm. "You know," I said, "you could assign somebody to watch my house instead. Isn't that what manpower is for?"

"You'd be just as hemmed in as you'll be here, only much less pleasantly. An' why make yourself an easy target? Our friend the note sender knows that address. At least give 'im a workout."

He rang the doorbell. Beth was all burbling surprise and smiles. It was obvious she hadn't seen the six o'clock news. Mackenzie introduced himself and improvised a weak story about the breakdown of both my car and my bathroom plumbing. He was heavy on the "Ma'ams" and the drawl, and another Yankee woman was suckered in.

Beth nodded, clucked, and tsked every time he said something unintelligible about my pistons or my S-curve leak. Her otherwise critical eyes went blind at the sight of anything ambulatory and male that might get me to do simultaneous carpooling with her.

Mackenzie leaned close to Beth and whispered, *sotto voce*. I heard his voice, heavy with concern, say words like "depressed," "shock of Liza," and "not to be left alone." Beth, who adored sick strays, went on red alert. The prospect of keeping her kid sister from ending it all was visibly thrilling.

"We'll stay with her constantly," Beth said in a stage whisper. I again had the feeling I had evaporated, or left the premises without knowing it. "She won't be alone for a minute."

I'd be cushioned by my lovely relatives, and I'd die of suffocation and boredom, instead.

"Take care," Mackenzie said. "I'll try to stop by."

"Listen here, Chipper—"

"Wrong." He closed the door behind him.

"What a *nice* man," Beth said. "Nice" isn't a word I relish, not for days, not for weather, and not for what's-his-name.

"And so attractive," she added, my subtle sister. She

liked that theme so much she played it over and over as she guarded me. Even Horse, the resident beast, was solicitous. He sat on my feet the entire night.

But I was too tired to react. Three cups of strong coffee with Beth couldn't stop my yawns or bring the circulation back into my limbs. I excused myself and went to the guest room, weighing the consequences of sleeping in my clothing. I couldn't remember if my mother had warned against it—what if Prince Charming finally found you and you were fully dressed like Sleeping Slob? I wondered if Mackenzie's given name was "Charming." Charming Knight? I wondered if I was indeed having a breakdown.

I've never understood why they call this the temperate zone. It is anything but. With weather ranging from below zero to one hundred degrees, it should be called the schizoid belt.

But every so often, with totally intemperate zest, a day blooms with a nearly painful beauty. It's a day for believing your lover's promises, for rediscovering humanity and feeling kinship with it, for deciding not to join the Sun Belt defectors just yet.

Saturday was one of those. I looked out the guest room window at a sincerely blue sky dotted with cartoon fluffs of clouds. Such a spring day promises a mind-boggling, glorious summer. I'd lived long enough to know that this promise is a bald-faced lie. Still, days like this are so sweet, prior knowledge becomes questionable. This is a brand-new beginning, and anything's possible.

The delicious pale-green-and-growing air was even in the shower and on my toothbrush, and I floated down to the kitchen in a euphoric haze.

Beth was all smiles. Then she looked worried.

"Karen and I have to run an errand. Sam will be with you, okay?"

I was tempted to stop this nonsense about my mental health, to tell her the real reason I was here. But that would probably impair *her* mental health, so I drank my coffee with only a nod for comment. I was happy to be unmonitored. Sam was not the most loquacious of men, and I would be left on my own to communicate with nature and myself. It would also be a reprieve from sisterly talk about Mackenzie's beauty and eligibility. From all talk, for that matter.

And I needed to stay undistracted. The breeze outside had cleared my mind, and I was positive that today I'd figure out what had been going on in my life and in Liza's and Eddie's. Maybe all those people were right and I did know something. Maybe I could even find out what it was. I happily waved good-bye to Beth and Karen before putting on a sweater and taking my coffee out to the flagstone patio behind the house.

I was, however, definitely being tailed. Sam silently joined me, settling on the wrought-iron chair next to mine. A robin hopped very close to our feet before fluttering to a more prudent vantage point.

Sam cleared his throat. "Mandy, can we talk?"

The day was filled with surprises. "Sure, Sam, what about?"

He cleared his throat again. Even in a worn-out sweater, Sam looks like a man in a vest and starched shirt.

"I know about it," he said.

At least seven recent and embarrassing possible "its" flashed across my mind, none of which I'd be eager to have my brother-in-law "know."

"You'll have to be more specific," I said in my most ladylike tones.

"I know why you're really here. I didn't want to worry Beth with it, but while you two were having coffee last night, I watched the late news. I saw you. Another murder, Mandy?"

"Oh, God, Sam, I can't control these impulses! What am I to do?"

The robin returned, staring quizzically. Maybe we were the first sign of spring for him, too.

Sam was also staring. "I didn't mean to imply that you were in any way involved in the commission of the crimes!"

I wondered if Sam ever cursed, muffed a sentence, or loused up his grammar.

"It was a joke," I said quietly. "I know you didn't mean it that way, and I don't know why I keep finding corpses. It's been horrible, and I'm terrified. But I hate to ruin this glorious day by dwelling on it."

"So, instead, you're dwelling in it. My dwelling, that is." Sam allowed a cautious chuckle at his own brand of witticism. For Beth's sake, I would like to think there's a secret, volcanic center to Sam. He's the kind of man who could probably commit endless crimes with impunity, because nobody'd be able to describe him. He's a lot of 'sort ofs'—sort of tall, sort of sandy hair—and, now that I think of it, lots of "nices," too—nice features, nice build, nice guy. Run that one through an Identikit, I dare you.

The door slammed, and Horse galumphed over to sit on my feet. "Mackenzie thinks I'll be safe in the bosom of my family. He doesn't think I should be seen with him, because then the murderer will think I know something."

"Wouldn't the, uh, culprit, think it anyway?"

"We prefer not thinking about that possibility."

"But still ..."

HER. HIM. YOU. A sterling example of clear communication. I pulled my sweater more closely around me, then I looked up. I could blame my sudden shivers on the moody sky, which had clouded over. "The uncertain glories of an April day," I said, noting how the colors of every new blade of grass and bud had gone dark. "Which reminds me, I have a test to write."

Our coffee and conversation were both finished, and without a word, we went back inside.

"I won't, of course, say anything about this matter to Beth." Sam went into his study. I walked into the library and found a soft leather-bound edition of *The Collected Works of Wm. Shakespeare*. Wm.'s words were barely legible on see-through paper. I thumbed through *Macbeth*, trying to remember the substance of our class discussions. But all I remembered was murder and guilt and bloody hands.

I decided that perhaps more caffeine would activate my professional brain cells. I went back to the kitchen. The coffee maker was empty, and ignoring the fact that this was a four-star kitchen, I opted for instant. I turned on the burner under the copper teakettle and stared at it as if it were an oracle.

Sam walked in with his empty cup. "What are you doing?" he asked.

"Making refills. Thinking."

"It's dangerous to think hunched over a teakettle. You could get burned."

"Ah, lately I've learned that you can get burned a lot of ways. But you're right. I'm keeping it from boiling, anyway."

We settled down to wait for the kettle to whistle. I made table talk. "Sam, judging from your experience, why do people commit murder?"

Sam looked startled and nervous. "That's hardly my

area of the law, Amanda. Contracts are quite different." Always cautious, he reconsidered what he'd said.
"Well, perhaps not. I'd assume that people do everything, including murder, because they want something
that somebody else has or controls."

"Liza's most valuable possession," I said, "was Hayden Cole, if I may characterize their relationship with
such unflattering terms." I was beginning to sound like
my brother-in-law. "And now, considering who else
would want that possession, and want it a great deal—"

Sam shook his head disapprovingly. "Let the police
handle this, Amanda. It's fruitless for us to speculate
without having all the information, isn't it? Don't upset
yourself with—"

"I'm not upset. I'm puzzled." Well, so it wasn't exactly honest, but it was kind. Sam didn't want to baby-
sit for a deranged sister-in-law. And for Sam, behavior
a level above comatose is dangerously out of line. "Do
you like Hayden Cole?" I asked.

"I've told you I know the man only casually. Why?"

"Frankly, I don't like him. He's plastic, artificial. A
good copy of something. You know how Gertrude Stein
said, 'There's no "there" there'? That's how he is."

"I know what you're suggesting, but I think you're
wrong. He's reserved and undemonstrative, but he's
human, Amanda."

I felt properly chastised. I know that Hayden has
feelings. It's just frustrating not to be able to fathom
what they are.

I busied myself with turning powder into coffee.
Sam accepted his refilled cup and smiled. "I'll get back
to work now," he said.

"Contracts are so clean, aren't they? People spell out
what they want in black and white. Nothing's hidden,
secret, explosive."

Sam sighed and paused at the kitchen doorway. I wasn't sufficiently merry for him to leave me in good conscience. So I smiled and winked. "Enough of this gloom, right, Sam? You're inspiring me. I'll get work done, too. I'm giving a test on *Macbeth* Monday, and I haven't written it yet. Now that would have been a great court case, wouldn't it? Who, ultimately, was the guilty party? If you think Fate is directing you, are you guilty? Is anyone ever *the* guilty party? I think I'll use that for my first question."

"You're all right, aren't you?" Sam said, so I readjusted my manic level.

"Sure. It's hard not thinking about what's happened, though. Before Monday, the only murders I knew about were in between book covers."

"Of course," Sam said. "Try not to let it get you, though."

"That's precisely what I'm trying," I muttered as he left.

Horse lumbered in. "Does anything make sense to you, dog? What's your theory?" He tried to sit on my feet, but I walked out to the garden and he shambled alongside. "Horse, what is your considered opinion?"

He looked up and lifted his ears in a splendid dumb-dog imitation of great concentration. He pondered the question, remained stymied, and opted for ankle-licking when I settled down in the rejuvenated sun-shine. Then he gave up the pretense of thought. His weight blanketed my feet, and after a moment, I heard his light snores.

I sipped coffee and flipped through Beth's volume of Shakespeare. I would indeed ask a question about guilt. "If you were to judge the events in *Macbeth*," I began.

"I have new shoes!" Karen was suddenly in front of me.

"Did we frighten you?" Beth said. "You look startled."

"I was concentrating. I didn't hear you." I considered how easily a person could sneak around a house
set in green padding, protected by a dog who would
only catch somebody in order to sit on his feet.

"Sorry we were so long. But we were near the shoe
store and Karen needed new tennies. So, unfortunately, did every other child in the entire area. I'll start
lunch now."

"Thanks, Beth, but I'll pass. I'm enjoying the sunshine, and I'm not hungry."

"Now, now, loss of appetite isn't healthy. Unless," she
said, "it's from love, of course." She waited in vain for
a response. "Stay where you are," she then continued.
"We'll eat out here. Everything's ready. Cheer up,
Amanda. Life must go on."

Her attempts to raise my spirits made me almost as
depressed as I was supposed to be.

Karen filled the time by demonstrating the variety of
gymnastic feats possible with her new red shoes. In
between her shouts and jumps, I scribbled away at my
test. "Whom would you consider guilty? Macbeth?
Lady Macbeth? Both? How important was the influence
of the witches' prophecies?" I wondered how Liza would
have answered the question. She'd had some interesting
ideas about guilt and responsibility, as I recalled.

"Ready or not, here we come!" Beth carried a tray of
food and led a small parade. I should have guessed. It
wasn't Sam, trailing her with a pitcher of lemonade and
a tray of glasses, who put the flush in her cheeks.

"Karen," she said in an unnaturally high melodic
mode, "come meet Aunt Mandy's friend, Officer Mackenzie."

"C.K.," he corrected her, putting a basket of home-made bread on the table.

The Wymans were too polite to question the man's lack of names.

Lunch was delicious, if boring during the spell while Karen assumed that we had convened to see her new shoes, and consequently discussed them at length, along with who else was similarly shod in school, and what stylistic variations were possible.

But it perked up when Beth began burbling about the evening's plans. I had more or less assumed we would gather around the tube, or do simultaneous silent reading. But no. "It's only a *local* carnival, of course," she said, "very suburban, I guess, but it's fun. And important for a whole group of charities out here. We all combine in this one effort. I'm sure Amanda will enjoy herself. And why don't you stop by, too, Officer—ah, C.K.?"

Mackenzie looked mildly taken aback, startled. "The, ah, Main Line Charities Carnival?" he asked.

"Yes!" She was thrilled; she was delighted. I mean I was surprised myself that he knew about some rinky-dink local fair, but Beth, looking for omens and signs that Mackenzie was my intended, was astounded. Delirious. "You've heard about our little event! What an amazing coincidence!"

Mackenzie nodded. "Some of Amanda's, ah, friends —the people at the Playhouse—are helping out. Their sponsor, Sissie Bellinger, seems to have involved them as clowns, or somethin'. And Hayden Cole's the auctioneer. Something like that?"

"Oh. Of course," Beth said, considerably subdued. The Unmentionable Case led to the fair, and its lights had dimmed somewhat.

"So you're plannin' to go and take Amanda," Mackenzie said quietly. He didn't sound thrilled.

"Oh, this isn't some wild kind of event that would upset her," Beth said with a chuckle. "Besides, we wouldn't leave her at home alone. And I promised to man the food booth for two hours, and Sam was going to take care of Karen. Unless you, of course, would be here to keep her company."

This was becoming fun. I waited. Mackenzie could either come clean and tell my sister that I was not suffering from depression but from danger, or be my date himself tonight.

"Tell you what," Mackenzie said. "I'll just clean up some paperwork and drop by the fair myself. Buy you some cotton candy, Karen."

I couldn't believe that he had chosen none of the above.

Sam excused himself and went back to work.

I stood to help clear the dishes. "No, no," Beth said. "Relax. Karen will help me."

Obviously, in Beth's campaign strategy, it was leave-the-lovers-alone time.

"I want to show C.K. how springy my shoes are!"

Beth frowned, then erased it. In order to cleanse the world of single females, married females in the presence of unmarried males present domesticity as the most blissful and placid of stages. So when Beth spoke, her voice was rich with maternal honey. "Later, sweetie," she told her daughter. "Right now, Mommy could use your help." Beneath the sugar was the steel of an Oberfuehrer's directive.

Karen is a bright child. She walked off, very springily, carrying three forks and some napkins, promising to return very soon.

Mackenzie pushed his chair back and slouched down

on it. "I've never seen you in sunshine before," he said pleasantly. "You should wear it more often. Bet you tan and look almost Eurasian with those cheekbones. Except for the red in your hair."

"Cut it."

"Ah'm complimentin' you. Some women require artificial light. They're limited. You aren't."

"Why not concentrate on keeping my skin intact instead of worrying about how it should be illuminated."

"You mean about tonight? What was I supposed to do? I knew about the damned thing because I have to be there, along with the whole cast of characters—except you, I had hoped. I didn't know your sister was involved."

"In something called Main Line Charities? You could have bet on it."

He shrugged. He seemed remarkably nonchalant about putting me in mortal peril. I wished he didn't look so damned pretty with the sunshine bopping off the silver sprinkles in his curls, highlighting some hitherto unnoticed freckles on his cheekbones.

He rocked the wrought-iron chair dangerously. "You have a marked tendency to overreact," he said. "Tonight's no big deal unless suburbanites frighten you. The more I think about it, the better this sounds. You'll be surrounded by hundreds of normal, charitable people. Maybe somebody will talk to you, say something interestin'. I'll redeputize you. Sam 'n' Beth and me, we'll never leave you alone. I'd rather you were there than here, alone. Unless you want me to see if I could get a police guard." He shrugged.

I considered my options and chose the populated fair. "What is it you'll do there?" I asked him.

"Lurk, menace, be stealthy. Make deductions. Maybe help Beth serve coleslaw. Raymond's been on my back. Suspects I'm devotin' overmuch time to tangential aspects of the case. Like you. He also does not wish to appear tonight. Says a man of his complexion cannot be inconspicuous on the Main Line."

"I am not a tangent."

"I'll be officially free at eleven, but until then, it'll be a pretty boring evening. Now—anything else you need to know? Aside from my name, of course."

"I need to know everything, so I can behave intelligently. I want to know everything you know."

"Oh, boy," he said, stretching himself out so that his sitting position was more like that of a log propped against the chair. "I know lots of stuff. I know that salt was once used as currency by the Chinese. I know that you shouldn't ignore the potential of household ammonia. I know how to convert stuff into metrics. And I know that even as we speak, Beth is considering color schemes for summer weddings and peeking out at us from time to time. I know—"

"You don't know when to quit. About the murders, C.K. What do you know that I don't?"

"Oh, that. Well, I know that Sissie's divorce became final three weeks ago, after long and fierce fighting about money of hers that Mr. Bellinger had permanently misplaced." Mackenzie stopped and concentrated on chewing ice cubes.

"So she isn't rich, and she isn't married."

"And she wasn't able to be openly on the market when Hayden went shopping for a wife. But now, she's very able to do what she pleases. And she has a remarkable incentive to do something."

"It's amazing what you turn up when you do some work, Mackenzie."

"What do you think I do when I'm not with you? Fantasize? Anyway, Sissie's status doesn't answer anything. There are other fat cats around for her to snare."

"But the legwork's been done with Hayden. And let's be honest, Sissie would make a better running mate. She belongs in his circle, and Liza didn't. That quarrel between Liza and Sissie last Sunday, it was probably about that. Sissie was pushing, harder and harder, to get the competition out and away. She said something to me—one of her damned half sentences—about a promise to finish the run and leave town. She meant Liza, I'm sure. But I don't understand why at all." I shook my head, still confused.

Beth reemerged from the house. "Hate to interrupt you—but how does a plate of ice cream sound?" She didn't sit down. That might have slowed our courtship by fifteen minutes.

Mackenzie tipped his chair back, chewing an imaginary corn stalk. "Why, Ma'am," he said. "That sounds amazin'ly fahn."

"You're overdoing it," I whispered, but "Ma'am" beamed.

"This is a *perfect* day for ice cream." He nodded agreement with himself. "That chicken of yours reminded me of the best days of home. And then we'd top it with ice cream."

"Aren't you mixing up your background?" I asked. "Shouldn't you be drawling about Creole goodies? Blackened redfish? Crayfish? Little French pastries?"

"Shows what Yankees know." He stood up and smiled again at Beth. "Let me help serve it," he said.

His accent was deepening and widening with every moment. He sounded more like Uncle Remus than a cum laude graduate of Rice.

"No, no," Beth answered. Of course. The young lovers were never to be parted.

"You can't carry three dishes," Mackenzie said.

She smiled and shook her head. "Two," she said. "Unlike my sister, I have to count calories. Besides, I have things to do about tonight." She all but bowed out backward.

Clever Bethy. She managed to keep to her diet and remind the unmarried visitor of the Single Sister's silhouette.

"You don't need to coat every word in molasses, Mackenzie. Beth is already hooked. Skip the Dixie overkill."

"Never hurts to sugar up the relatives," he said. "A Southern accent gives me an edge. Everybody up here thinks that the brain works in slow motion. They relax their guard."

"Listen, did we exhaust all the available information?" I asked. "I'm still more interested in what's going on than in ice cream."

"Like what? Ah'm an open book."

"Like do you know when Eddie died?"

"Between ten and eleven, thereabouts, Friday morning."

"Then I couldn't have—I didn't even know his last name at 10:00 A.M." I felt a meaningless, selfish, but nonetheless real sense of relief. "Then tell me, where was Sissy on Monday and Friday?"

"You favor her as a suspect? She has the most depressing alibi I've heard in a while. She was: (a) carpooling her son to school; (b) being a mother-helper in Petey's room; (c) having her hair washed. She was: (d) shopping for a green dress; (e) taking shoes to the cobblers; (f) seeing a printer about the carnival's auction list; (g) attending a meeting of the Friends of some disease—I can't remember... Do I have to go on? That might be out of order, but both days' schedules are like that. Little bits of action, nothin' related to anything else."

"Shh!" I pointed toward the house. If Beth heard him, she'd feel even more guilty about enjoying her life. "Anything else?"

"The bear. We x-rayed it, did an assay."

This was great, authentic cloak-and-dagger stuff. "What was inside?" I whispered.

"More bear. Nothing else."

Beth reappeared with two dishes. Each had three small scoops of ice cream, one chocolate, one vanilla, one strawberry. Just so everyone received satisfaction and high cholesterol. "Karen's taking a little nap," she said. "Resting up for the big evening."

The coast was clear. We could do what we liked. Beth, enormously pleased with her orchestration of the day, left again, beaming.

"Anything else you found?" I asked Mackenzie. I took a spoonful of chocolate and promised myself that I would not, absolutely would not, eat three scoops of ice cream.

"No, but there's something else we didn't find. Fingerprints. Not at Eddie's, either. It wasn't raining that time, so I'm not so sure about the raincoat-and-gloves theory. Also, nobody knows if anything's missing from Eddie's apartment. So that's some more noninformation."

"How about Hayden? The brunch?"

C.K. shrugged. "Far as we can tell, he was there from elevenish until three."

"So you consider him out of the running? Really out?" I ate some strawberry, then a few spoonfuls of vanilla.

"You're not hiding your disappointment very well. But all right. He's not completely covered, because for

almost two hours he excused himself to work on a
speech while the club had its business meeting. He
wasn't feeling great, didn't want to eat, and they had
failed to give him the precise time they needed his bod-
ily presence. He worked upstairs in an empty office."

"Says who?"

"His campaign manager. Don't say it—I'm not putting much weight on that. But so far, I don't have any
evidence that he left the place."

"Where was he on Friday morning?"

"In his study. Not to be disturbed by anyone. Not
even Mama."

"That's one weak alibi."

Mackenzie took a break from conversation to savor
his chocolate ice cream. "Raymond considers my chocolate obsession overcompensation for racial guilt," he
said when he had finished the scoop. "I wish somebody
hadn't thought it was cute to put me with Raymond."

"I *hate* to interrupt again, but I thought you might
like this." Beth carried a tray with frosty glasses, a
pitcher of iced tea with mint leaves, and a tray of home-
made cookies. She put it on the table between us and
filled the two glasses. Then, beaming, she retreated
once again while we both murmured thanks. I was beginning to feel like a Strasbourg goose.

"Where were we?" Mackenzie asked.

"With the perfect Mr. C.," I finally managed. "The
one who followed his infant schedule from birth,
crossed only at corners, and never cheated on an
exam."

"I'm still lookin' for some kind of motive, too. Maybe
he knew about Eddie?"

"You didn't leave! Goody," Karen said, having completed the shortest nap in recorded history. "I want to
show you my playhouse, C.K." She tugged at him,

urging him to the back of the garden where Sam had lovingly constructed a sort of earthbound tree house for his daughter. I wasn't invited to join them.

"One second," Mackenzie said. "Let me give your auntie something to read first." He extracted a fat square of yellow papers from the patch pocket of his corduroy jacket. "Here's something, maybe," he said in his decisive way. "Mrs. Nichols's contribution."

"You were there, too?"

"I get around, kiddo. I was there three times this week. Found this the second time. Tuesday morning. But don't get riled. We weren't for sure on the same team then, remember?"

"Come on," Karen said. I looked at the sheaf of thin second sheets, a carbon copy of a play called *Never Say Forever.*

There was a scrawled note about the title. "Please reconsider," it said. "Can't we at least try it *onstage*? This could help us both. Let me know soon. *Please*?" The last underlining was heavy enough to have ripped the tissue paper. I didn't need to look at the author's name typed below the title. I knew Gus's handwriting.

The stage directions didn't help. "Scene One: Interior of a run-down apartment. Stacks of old newspapers fill the corners. Opened cans, etc., stand on counter of Pullman kitchen. *Michael Fillmore*, age around forty, unshaven and homely, sits on unmade bed. He rises and crosses to small icebox, one arm hanging lifelessly and right leg dangling."

I didn't read the dialogue. I flipped through the pages, seeing enough that way. A young girl entered, described as "beautiful, in an earthy, unclassical way, as a Gypsy might be. Her clothing is flashy, unconventional."

Act One ended with them on the still-unmade bed.

"Well?" Mackenzie said when he had finally satisfied Karen and been released back to me.

"I felt like a voyeur. There are parts of a person that just aren't for public display."

"He was hopin' to have the whole thing displayed."

"Still, it's so sad."

"Maybe it's more than sad."

"I don't care. Even if it wasn't over for him emotionally. Even if—"

"That play could have turned his life around," Mackenzie said. "He'd be acting again. Safely, in a tailor-made part nobody could deny him. He would have a produced play to his credit. His whole life could have changed, gone nearer to where he'd once aimed for."

"Somebody else could have played the girl's part if Liza declined."

"Sure, but Winston's obsessed with her. Did you read the ending?"

I shook my head.

"The guy gets himself together, doesn't need her anymore. That's the good news. The bad news is he only finds that out after she dies."

"You're not saying—"

"Of course not."

"That must be what he wanted to talk to Liza about," I said. "Sunday night, then Monday morning." Oh, God, had he called her from school about the script? And had he gone there to reason with her and heard, instead, damning, destructive things? It wasn't just his artistic ego on the line in this; it was his life.

"I wasn't going to show you the script," Mackenzie said. "It is indeed private and painful, and it may be irrelevant. But I thought you'd be safer if you understood Gus a little better."

He was quiet for a moment. "Let's take these plates in," he said. I tagged along.

"You've got quite a daughter here," he told Beth.

"You've got quite a way with children," she answered. I knew that Beth hoped her daughter had driven Mackenzie to a feverish need for children of his own, children of the same basic gene pool as Karen. And I knew that Mackenzie knew that, and that made it bearable.

But I didn't listen to their mutual back patting. I thought about Gus, my good Gus who saw himself as a deformed, pathetic failure. Gus, still replaying his relationship and ending it, finally, unequivocally.

Beth busied herself at the sink, and Mackenzie took his attention off the gleaming kitchen counters. "One more thing," he said to me, too softly to be overheard. "When Winston visited Liza's mother Tuesday night, he was nervous about this script. Told her that Liza had borrowed it and it was needed immediately. She was afraid to say that the police had it. He made her search through Liza's room."

Of course, he might have simply wanted to keep it private. And of course, all his questions to me about what the police knew still could have been altruistic, concerned only about my welfare.

Beth turned off the water. "Do you think your husband would mind bein' disturbed?" Mackenzie asked her. "I have a question for him."

Beth was ready to grant Mackenzie anything, certainly something as easy as Sam. She didn't seem to wonder why he wanted the audience, but I did. I was sure he wasn't asking Sam about contracts or for my hand.

But when he came out of Sam's study, he offered a

smile and farewells instead of information. He didn't really kiss Beth's hand and ride off on a white charger, but you couldn't tell that from her expression.

"He's so attractive," she murmured.

I nodded, but I wasn't thinking about Mackenzie; I was thinking about murder. Why does someone kill? Because he wants something, Sam had said. Power, money, love. But it all finally boils down to self-defense. A person takes another's life because his own seems in danger. So the trick is figuring out what is seen as vital, essential to sustain life.

My flash of insight was as long-lived and illuminating as a firefly's light. I still knew nothing.

I thought, instead, about the night ahead. Something was going to happen. Something big. My mood —a combination of fear, intense interest, and anxious excitement—felt familiar. My skin had felt this tight and tingly before; my mind had been dizzied by "what ifs." Some other time, I had been unsteady on my feet, half running forward and half holding back. But since I'd never knowingly mingled with murderers before, what was this feeling and why was it so familiar?

And then I laughed out loud.

I'd felt this way most of my adolescence. The same eagerness and avoidance, prurient interest tinged with disbelief and fear, the same nervous, delighted speculation. I'd felt like this all that long waiting time between hearing the facts of life and getting a chance to try them out.

Fourteen

I ARRIVED AT THE CARNIVAL READY TO GIVE my all. But if the anxious excitement had been familiar, so was the letdown I now felt. In the same ancient past, the first boy to whom I'd offered my young self had nearly died of fear. I tend to rush things, tend to be disappointed, and tend not to learn anything from the experience.

The carnival grounds were nearly deserted. There was nobody to give my all or my anything to.

Instead, I helped Beth unwrap and stack several boxcar loads of hot dog rolls. I opened industrial-size jars of mustard and relish and filled trays with potato chips and coleslaw.

"Now, run along, you three," Beth insisted after a time, and heigh-ho, we finally went to the fair. Sam, Karen, and I milled around, checking the various offerings before the real crowds arrived.

I was impressed by the extravagance and size of what was, after all, a local fund-raiser. I had expected amateurish, homemade games, but this was a large, ambitious affair sprawling over several acres of a shopping center's street-side parking lot.

Which was not to say it was thrilling or even interesting for a long spell, as Sam and I tagged behind Karen and observed, or participated in, games with blow tubes and balloons, tiny fishing rods and goldfish, and a picture version of blackjack.

And then it became that time of evening when outlines grow fuzzy and I suspect I have contracted glaucoma. And suddenly, the lights went on.

"Ooooh, look!" Karen shouted as the scalloped umbrella of the merry-go-ground came alive with white sparklers and the ferris wheel spun in multicolored glory.

The mechanisms, spokes, engines, and gears disappeared, and only the glitter remained. We were suddenly in another place altogether, at a carnival real and true where nothing ordinary could happen. Karen wasn't the only one to sense the magic. People began arriving and filling the walkways.

"The sky jumper, Daddy," Karen said. "Can I go on it now, before everybody wants to?" We wandered over to a huge plastic bubble with a trampoline interior, and I held Karen's shoes as she bounced around inside of it. "Sam," I said, now that we were alone, "what did Mackenzie want to talk about today? Can you tell me?"

Sam looked surprised, but mildly, as was his wont. "Old history," he finally said. "Nothing particularly relevant, I should think. Something that happened in college, to be precise."

"To you?"

He shook his head and seemed to feel that answered my question.

I prodded. "So the two of you reminisced about the good old days?"

"They weren't good at all just then," Sam said. "The fellow in question hanged himself. In the upstairs bathroom of the fraternity house." He shook his head. "Horrible time. A few days before graduation. His, of course. I was only a freshman, a pledge. I had thought of him as the ideal, something to aim for. He was about to begin a military career in the Air Force. Good record, good-looking, popular, and he hanged himself three days before graduation."

"Why?"

"Nobody knew. They say he left a note for his folks."

"I mean, why would Mackenzie ask you about a dead fraternity brother?"

"I'm sure he had his reasons." Sam had an unbelievable lack of curiosity. "His questions were very specific."

Karen bounced out of the sky jumper, and I handed her the red canvas shoes. "Specific how?" I asked Sam. "What were they?"

Sam, who was now helping his daughter tie her laces, looked up at me and sighed. I could tell before he spoke that I had definitely exceeded his limits. Frankly, I was surprised he had told me anything. "You might want to ask your detective friend about it yourself," Sam finally said before returning to his paternal duties.

I stood corrected. And then, speaking of the devil, or detective, I saw my defender shuffling toward us, his shoulders slumped. "Havin' fun?" he asked pleasantly when he reached us.

"Oh, a keen time. Frankly, marking vocabulary tests is more exciting than this detective business."

Sam stood up, groaning like a geriatric case. "Hungry, you two? Karen needs sustenance."

"We'll join you at the food booth in a few minutes," Mackenzie said. It was the changing of the guard, and the Wymans walked off. "I brought you somethin'," he said. "Now that you're officially redeputized, you might want to feel more like a trained professional. We are expert in disguises, you know." He pulled a tangled plastic mess from his jacket pocket. "Voilà," he drawled, putting on heavy plastic eyeglasses supporting an enormous red nose and black mustache. "See? You'll wear this and be out of danger completely. People will rush to tell you secrets, never guessin' your true identity." He transferred the glasses and mustache to my face.

"It's hard to breathe in there, ah know," he said. "This is no line of work for snivelers."

"We're going to wander around like this?" I asked, sounding a lot like a duck.

"Not 'we.' You. Ah'm doin' a stint at the food booth. Impressin' your sister on company time."

"Sorry," I said, taking off the nose. "The mustache clashes with my hair. Before you split, could you tell me something? Why did you ask Sam about a fraternity brother of his?"

"Tell you what," he said as we walked the fairgrounds, dodging happy carnival-goers. "Try to figure it out while I serve. If you can't, I'll explain it all later. Clue—I used information you yourself gave me." We arrived at Beth's stand. He clicked his heels. "Mackenzie reporting, Ma'am. We also serve who only stand and serve."

Beth glowed as she explained the intricacies of manning the various scoops.

"I think I've got it," he said finally. "Why don't you take a break? You must be exhausted."

Beth looked bemused and very young. "I'd love a chance to look around," she said.

I knew what she planned to look at. My soul. Outside, in the shadow near the booth, she took my arm.

"He is a perfectly wonderful man," she said. "There aren't many like that. I do hope you're making the most of this opportunity."

"I worship the ground he walks on. I think of him night and day. I've never met anyone like him before." I knew I was setting myself up for further complications later, but my words made Beth so happy, it was worth it.

"Do not, however, plan the wedding yet," I added.

"I can't imagine what you're talking about."

"Do not push. Do not pass 'go.' Do not oversell."

"What on earth am I selling?"

"Coleslaw, because nothing else is on the market. Remember that." I walked back and ordered the works from Mackenzie, and then, anchored by Sam at my side, a sagging paper plate in one hand and Karen holding the other, I sauntered off.

"I want to ride the ferris wheel," Karen said. "Come up with me, Aunt Mandy?"

"I can't just now," I said, shoving the hot dog roll into my mouth. "I'm eating."

Her father offered to be her copilot. I walked beside them to the waiting line. I didn't even like looking up and seeing those little seats dangling and lurching, stopping and starting.

"Aunt Mandy's afraid," Karen said as we edged forward in line.

"I'm eating. I told you." I broke a single potato chip into four sections, chewing each one slowly.

"Fortunes?" a voice sang out. "Let the Gypsy read your palm. Fifty cents. Only fifty cents for charity."

She wore a black wig, heavy makeup, and a red satin gown recycled from a bordello. Without the beige hair and shotgun questions, Sissie Bellinger was hard to recognize.

"Fortune, Meester?" she asked Sam. "Geepsy weel read your palm." She tossed her head and stomped like Carmen. I knew why she hadn't gone far in the theater.

Sam smiled and pulled out more of his declining capital. "Why not?" he said. "Fortunes all around. On me."

The line moved up again. We'd be the next batch to fill up the ferris wheel. I could either be honest and admit my fears—and have them try to help me conquer them, or I could keep on eating. I chewed a single cube of relish.

Sissie wasn't terrifically inventive. She oohed and aahed at Karen's little hand. "I see travel in the sky in your future. Excitement."

"The ferris wheel!" Karen said with delight. Then even she caught on. "You can see we're in line! No fair!"

"Geepsy knows fortune from lines on your hand, little one," Sissie said. But she sighed and looked for something new. "Here, a strong lifeline, see? A long life. Adventures. Much love. But you have a strong will. You must listen to the wisdom of your parents. Always."

Karen scowled. She looked as if she might report the palmist to the Better Business Bureau.

Sissie polished her act for the grown-up clientele. "The line of the heart is not so long as the line of the head," she said to Sam. "You're a thinker. A deep man. And I see a good marriage here with much affection and kindness from this long heart line." She ran her fingers lightly over his palm. "But not altogether the thinker," she said with a low chuckle. She prodded the fleshy area near his thumb and suddenly remembered her accent. "Thees ees the mound of

Venus. For love." She chuckled again. "Yours ees very well developed."

And I would have sworn he'd gotten that puffiness from holding a pen tightly, but what did I know? It was an intriguing new aspect of Sam. He pursed his mouth in an attempt not to smile.

"Next," the guardian of the ferris wheel said. "Fill 'em up, folks. Come right along."

"You coming, Aunt Mandy?"

"I'm eating." I stepped away from the line as the others entered the boxy, teetering seats.

"I'll do yours now," Sissie announced.

"It's all right. I'll take a rain check. My palms are greasy anyway."

But Sissie grabbed my free hand, laughing and tossing her acrylic tresses. "Your brother-in-law, he paid for eet," she said. I still clutched the plastic fork.

She shook her head slowly, making her gold-hoop earrings sway. "Umm." She turned my palm up with a surprisingly strong grip. The fork hurt my fingers.

"The head here is not so well developed as the heart." She looked up at me from under her false lashes. "You are the type to leap before looking? To become involved in things before you understand them, then?"

"Perhaps," I said lightly. No flattering sexual surprises in my palm, I guessed. Sissie kept her pale brown eyes on mine and her fingernail dug into my underdeveloped head line, if that was what that wrinkle was.

"Yes," she said, looking back at my palm. "Yes, you do. You interfere. You don't think. It is a dangerous trait, one to be avoided."

"In general, Sissie? Or in some specific instance you'd like to mention?"

"In every instance," she said slowly. "Look." The smell of camphor floated off her black wig. "The lifeline." She ran her fingernail down the curvy line near my thumb. "It breaks. Poof! Soon, perhaps."

I looked. She was right about the break, although no specific termination date was imprinted. "Wow," I said. "You must have majored in palmistry at Bryn Mawr. But what does it mean?"

"What do you think it means? Stay out of things that don't concern you. Don't make things worse than they are. Save your life." My hand twitched, or flinched, trying to break her grip. "Good," she said, "you are finally nervous. Perhaps your head is beginning to work as it should."

"The fork is beginning to work its way through my skin, Sissie. Let go. It's your hand that's twitching. Or showing."

She stared at me, still clenching my hand. Her nail and the fork tines dug into my flesh. Maybe she was trying to elongate my lifeline as an act of charity.

"Sissie," I said softly, "what is it that you want?"

"Only what I deserve," she snapped. "Nothing more." She threw my hand away like a crumpled napkin and swished off, threadbare red satin and thick black hair merging into the crowd.

I looked down. My abbreviated lifeline smarted from her claws. It ended with the half-moon imprint of a nail. "This is where you get off," it seemed to say.

I wasn't supposed to be playing sleuth, only gathering information, but I knew that my encounter with Sissie would sound like much less than it had been, so I began my own deductions, despite Mackenzie's warnings.

The ferris wheel crowd returned to earth. "Forty minutes, folks, before the auction" sounded over the loudspeaker. "All booths and amusements will close in forty minutes. There's still plenty of popcorn and fun, so step right up."

It was a siren call to Karen, who obviously had been given an unlimited pocketbook. "I want to go to the Magic Maze of Mystery," she said. "Before it closes."

"I don't think you'll like it," I protested. The kid slept with a Sunny Bug night-light and the hall door wide open. She didn't seem the type for even fake, hokey scares.

"Nicholas Nelson went through. He said it was okay. He said there's a gorilla in there who's really his father."

"Sam, do you think she should—" But Sam looked oddly distracted. "I'll, ah, meet you there, or at its exit," he said. "I have to—excuse me, please. Here." He handed over the little cardboard tickets he'd bought and walked toward a Porta-John at the edge of the parking lot. He'd been a brave man to add the ferris wheel to the food concession's offerings.

"Please, Aunt Mandy? It won't scare you."

"I'm not worried about me." We walked over to the sidewalk and the shops. Next to a place called Denim Heaven, a vacant store had been boarded and blackened. Above the dark window an old sign still read "Fresh Fish."

"They've done an incredible job," the volunteer said while ripping up our little tickets of admission. "The family who runs the theatrical supply house downtown took the whole thing on themselves. Not your run-of-the-mill fun house. You'll love it."

I doubted that. I think fear should be a rare and unwelcome intruder, not an invited guest. I avoid horror movies and terrifying novels, and I cannot understand how haunted houses and chambers of horrors could be considered attractions. But I had used up my

cowardice allowance at the ferris wheel. The old fish
store didn't look too big, so I sighed, decided that this
was more likely to be short and boring than anything
else.

Karen, jumping up and down with eagerness, took
my hand and we entered the black-painted door.

"AHEEYAH!"

That was hello in Magic Maze talk. It was also a new
sort of instant aerobics. I waited until my heart resumed something like its normal pace and tried to adjust my eyes to the black void.

"Welcome," the electronic voice crackled. "The
Magic Maze of Mystery needs more victims. Try to
find your way through. Just try!" The voice found the
idea hilarious and convulsed into delirious shrieks.

My eyes did not adjust. There was nothing to adjust
to. This was the darkness of the blind, total and im-
penetrable.

"Where are you, Karen?" I whispered. We had
dropped our hands with our opening screams. I put
my hands out to find her. "Oh, excuse me!" I pulled
my hand back from the spongy touch of someone's
generous bosom. But no one answered. I put my hand
out again. The Maze was lined with soft, padded walls.
And they were close together, so that miles of pitch-
black corridors could fit inside a little fish store.

I should have chosen the ferris wheel.

"Karen?" I said, taking a step. My foot sank into
dark softness. The floors were also padded, alive,
yielding and terrible.

I hated the place. I yearned for the former fish market, for white, gleaming cases and silvery skins and
hard fluorescent lights. I lost my bearing with no solid
walls, no solid earth, to step on. "Karen?" I repeated.

My voice was muffled by the padding, drowned out by another scream on the sound system.

The Maze was hot. Padded and stifled and musty. "Karen?" She had disappeared into the stuffing.

"Here," a small voice whispered. "Here." I took two more tentative steps on the unsure ground and bumped into her. She took my hand, and step by step, arms outstretched, we made our way around a corner.

"BOO! I'LL GET YOU!" The recorded voice wasn't nearly as frightening as was the total absence of light.

Karen finally remembered that she hated the dark. "I don't like this," she whimpered. "Carry me?"

I theorized that one pair of legs, even carrying a little girl, could speed up this trip. The going was difficult with only one free arm and Karen's legs bouncing against my thighs. The padded floor felt far away. I couldn't remember where my legs ended.

We turned and twisted along, hopefully not backtracking. Karen controlled herself, whimpering softly until wet, wormlike tendrils dripped across our faces. At that, she screamed, directly into my right ear.

"It's spaghetti!" I shouted, pushing us around yet another turn.

"GGGRRRRRRRHAH!" shouted a furry gorilla, illuminated in a burst of green light. "YEEEOWRL!"

"You're Nicholas's father!" Karen screamed. "You aren't scary! You aren't! You aren't a gorilla at all!" Nevertheless, she put both her hands around my neck in a stranglehold. "Run!" she shouted.

But I couldn't, not on the soft flooring, not with my heavy burden. "Karen, we must be near the end of this place. Could you walk the last few feet? Please?"

She sniffled, braced herself, and let me put her down. Her grip on my hand was like a vise. Between

Sissie's claws and the fork a while ago, and Karen now, I figured I was going to have to discard that hand by the end of the evening. We moved even more slowly as Karen fumbled along, moving only after she had tested the ground several times.

"YEEEK!" the walls screamed.

"I don't like this place," Karen said again and again.

"We're near the exit." There was no sign that my assumption was correct. I had no idea where I was heading, or if I was merely retracing my steps. I groped along the side wall, formulating complaints to the people who'd designed this terrifying and dangerous place.

Then suddenly, my hand missed, cut through empty air. No wall. Nothingness. I groped in the other direction. More nothingness. I lost all sense of direction and felt lost in an enormous void. Where were its edges? Where was the way out?

"YEEEE!" the building said. "YEY-YAH-HEHE-HEHE!" It didn't stop, so that I was deafened and dislocated. My breathing accelerated as I fought off panic, my free arm flailing, my whole body frozen in place, afraid to move and fall, become lost—

And then a red burst of pain exploded in the dark. Something heavy hit my neck. I screamed—but the invisible speakers outdid me. I lurched forward, dropping Karen's hand, struggling to regain my footing and not to cry.

"I hate this!" Karen screamed, but I could barely hear her.

"YOU'LL NEVER LEAVE MY MAZE!" the electronic maniac screamed.

"Mommy!" Karen wailed.

What in God's name had slugged me? That couldn't be part of the tour. There was something or someone nearby, and I had no idea of the size of our arena or the location of my attacker. My impulse was to curl up, hide, become too small a target.

"I want my mommy!" Karen repeated.

I was afraid to say anything at all.

"YEEEEEAH!" the walls screamed.

There was no way to avoid whatever had cracked me on the neck, and I couldn't stand there in the dark. I groped and stumbled until I found Karen, who screamed and then grabbed on to me. I pulled her, propelling us in the direction I hoped was forward.

And directly into a solid mass of flesh that pushed back, hard.

"MYSTEREEEE!" the walls screamed.

"What the—" a voice shouted.

"MOMMY!" Karen continued.

A large hand grabbed me, pulled me, pushed me. For the second time in my life—and in the week—I instinctively raised my knee.

I heard a groan.

The hand fell away.

"GET ME OUT OF HERE!" Karen screamed, filling the dark, filling my mind.

"DON'T SCREAM!" I answered, rationally or not, and I ran forward blindly, tripping on the mushy padding, pulling both of us down.

I heard heavy breathing.

"GET UP!" I screamed.

And then I saw the three-sided slit of light that had to mean a door. And finally, a dim red light above it that spelled safety, E-X-I-T.

"Run!" I shouted. "That way!" And despite the spongy footing, we galloped to the back door.

I didn't stop until I was outside on the firm cement behind the Maze, surrounded by parked cars and streetlights. It was a fish store in a shopping center, I told myself. But it had been all my childhood night-mares boiled in a cauldron until it condensed into those noises, the lost floors and walls and sense of direction, the menacing stranger. It had been the whole last week, bound up in a dark package that held nothing normal, nothing solid, and nothing that made sense.

"Let's find your daddy," I said, but the back door opened, and now that I was back in a normal world, I wanted to see what manner of monster emerged.

It wasn't a monster. It was the Hunchbacked Clown of Notre Dame. A strange doubled-over figure in bright patchwork pantaloons and whiteface craned its neck in my direction. "Mandy!" It said from its crouched position. "What are you doing here? Christ, you wouldn't believe what happened in there."

I stared at Gus. My neck still hurt. It felt as if some-body had wanted to break it.

"I bumped into somebody," he said, "and Jesus..."

I guess I should have confessed, explained, but I was physically sore and mentally troubled. The vague, enormous fear I'd had inside the Maze had diminished into a hard little question mark.

"Why were you in there, Gus?" I was going to re-quire a fantastic answer. Like me, Gus was not the type to consider using up a break from his work for a dash into a midnight-dark padded cell. Unless he had seen me, followed me, almost managed to break my neck.

"Petey," he said with a sigh.

"What's that? Code?"

"That's that." A young blond boy came out by him-self, smiling.

"Petey!" Karen exclaimed with delight.

"Sissie asked me to take him through," Gus said

slowly, wincing. "I don't know why I agreed. I wish I could rub where it hurts."

"I stayed in all by myself," Petey Bellinger said.

"That was fun, wasn't it?" My hypocritical niece's voice was blithe.

"Yeah," Petey said. "Want to do it again? I wasn't scared, but some people screamed."

"They must be babies," Karen said with scorn.

"I didn't think you'd be out this soon." The appearance of Sam was like a lighthouse beam in a storm. He no longer appeared dull, predictable, unexciting. Or rather, he was all those things, and they were wonderful. The action-packed life was not for me. I was in pain. I no longer trusted my friends. I felt ill and confused and over my head, and I didn't want to stay at this party any longer.

"Gus Winston," Gus said, introducing himself.

"Ah, yes, Mandy's friend." Sam shook Gus's hand.

I didn't know anything anymore. I felt much younger and less worldly-wise than Karen, and I wanted a night-light and a bedtime story that ended happily.

Fifteen

C.K. WAS DISHING CHIPS AND HOT DOGS when we joined him. "How's it going?" he asked casually, oblivious of anything but his munchies.

I waited until the gang drifted away after purchasing jelly beans, chocolate chip cookies, and more soda. "This is not where the action is," I hissed. "Or have you changed careers, Cyril?"

"Wrong, and did somethin' happen?"

"Yes! Or, well, I don't know. I thought so, but..." It had been a dark, empty building, an open space without walls. It could have been what Gus said it was, an unfortunate collision of two people desperate to get out. I didn't want to implicate Gus any further. On the other hand, my neck still hurt.

"Why don't you go enjoy yourself now?" Beth said, dancing over to her protégé. "We're closing soon, anyway. Go on, now; you've done more than your fair share." She beamed up at Mackenzie and he bowed, wiping a strand of coleslaw off his watch.

"We'll see you at the auction," he said, and Beth nodded happily at the way he was blending right in.

I told Mackenzie about the Maze and about my lamentable fortune-telling session with Sissie. "I'm a lousy detective," I admitted. "I didn't learn anything new, except about the possibilities of my pulse rate. Aren't I supposed to be hearing things that will clarify everything?"

"Oh, yes," he said. "That's how it always goes. You start talking about the meanin' of life, and somebody says, 'Why, I was thinkin' the same thing while pouring boiling water on a fellow's face yesterday.'"

"The field's not exactly narrowing, is it?"

"Nope. Still the big three, I guess. Cole's here, by the way. Over where they're setting up the auction. He agreed to play auctioneer a long while back, and he's fulfillin' his contract. Everyone back at the food booths seems to think that makes him some kind of saint, the way he's holdin' up and hidin' his grief."

I realized how many parts of my body were either exhausted or in active pain. "C.K., I'm carnivaled out," I said. "Why don't we go sit on the chairs in the auction area—we can observe the suspect and rest the feet."

Mackenzie didn't put up a fight or insist that he hadn't yet ridden the ferris wheel or visited the house of mystery. We walked between the booths and the balloon men toward the supermarket.

"Sissie said my heart was more strongly developed than my mind," I told him.

"And I thought palm reading was bunk."

The auction area was a study in motion. I watched a plump lady in purple crease, then place a leaflet on each and every folding chair.

"Shall I tell her she's doomed, Claudius?" I whispered.

"Nope to both your questions. She's happy."

But she wasn't for long. A renegade breeze, perhaps left over from March, waited until she was done, then raced across the chairs. The airborne programs flapped aimlessly, then, like a flock of pigeons, settled to earth in a haphazard pattern.

"Nothing's going right!" the lady shrieked, dashing from spot to spot, clutching her wounded papers. I collected a few dozen myself and handed them to her.

"*Now* what can I do?" she wailed.

"Why not hand them out as people arrive?" I suggested.

She looked at me with awe, ready to grant me the Nobel Prize. "Of course," she said, visibly regaining her will to live. "It's just been too much. Half the items arrived late. Janine forgot the gavel, and now it's cold and windy. I wonder if it'll rain and ruin everything. These things shouldn't be in April, but all the schools have June fairs."

The wind had died down, but not away. My blouse no longer felt like adequate cover. I smiled at the woman as she thanked me again, and I looked for Mackenzie. He was studying a large, ornately framed painting that rested against a folding chair.

"Are you, ah, going to bid on that?" I asked.

"Why would someone get rid of this?" he asked, making me very nervous about our aesthetic compatibility.

"Because it's hideous?"

"Sure," he agreed, "but who'd ever let this monstrosity into his house unless it was an ancestor's portrait? And then, who'd sell it off? And who'd buy it? Now that's a real mystery."

I was acutely bored with his vague musings. "Speaking of which, you promised you'd tell me what you talked to Sam about."

"You haven't puzzled it out?"

"No. I was busy getting threatened and pushed around in the dark. Go on, nameless, explain."

He put the ugly painting back in place, and pushing his hands into the pockets of his windbreaker, he stood, rocking slightly on his heels, looking disappointed. "You had all the relevant facts, you know. You told me Sam had gone to Franklin and Marshall. And you knew our friendly auctioneer went there for three years and had been Sam's fraternity brother. He transferred to Penn his senior year." He waited, then sighed. "You still don't get it?"

"Skip the gloating, okay?"

"It's hard, but I'll try. What you said this afternoon is true. Our man was the kid with the good citizenship badges. In a lifetime of completely predictable, safe behavior, his transfer is the single exceptional act. Why, after three good years, leave a college your family endowed? Anything out of character bothers me, so I tried checking it out. But Cole left voluntarily, spent the summer making up nontransferable courses, and then completed undergraduate school roughly on time."

"So far, it's less than mind-bending."

"Sorry. But use your common sense—there has to be a reason for leaving, and if there's no official one, then you look around unofficially. Like to his fraternity brothers. You kind of handed Sam to me on a platter, and I thank you."

"Miss! Oh, Miss, if you aren't busy, *could* I *possibly* ask you to fold the rest of the fliers?" It was my friend in purple, so flushed with confusion that her cheeks clashed with her clothing. "It wouldn't take much time, and I'd be so eternally grateful."

While I tried to think of a believable excuse, and I

pondered how much eternal gratitude was worth, Mackenzie signed both of us on. We walked over to the folding chairs, sat down, and began creasing and stacking, to the enormous relief of the purple woman.

"You were saying..." I said once we were alone with our programs. I waited. I tried again. "I handed Sam to you on a platter?"

"Uh-huh."

"*And*...?"

"And I am grateful."

"No! *More*, Mackenzie. Why are you grateful?"

"Because he was helpful, after some judicious prompting. Then, based on what he remembered, I called the school again and was able to ask specific questions and get answers."

I shivered from either the damp breeze or from unwelcome anticipation. Whatever the news was, it was definitely decades old, yellow, and cracked around the edges. And I remembered Sam saying that the old times Mackenzie had asked about couldn't be called "good."

"There was a hush-hush campus scandal during Hayden's junior year," C.K. said. "A senior was caught in flagrante delicto and he hanged himself."

"That's why he did it? Sam said he never knew why. But that's no reason. Even before people admitted it, people did have sex. Why kill yourself over it? And F&M isn't some fundamentalist Puritan school. One of my most liberated friends graduated from it, and she said—"

"She wouldn't have been able to say anything about F&M back when Sam and Hayden were there. It was all men then."

"Oh. And the sex partner wasn't imported from the outside world?"

Mackenzie nodded.

"So the dead boy had been with...?"

"A fraternity brother. The man who found them tried to shut down the whole fraternity first."

"And are you saying that the other man was—"

"Well, the school wouldn't say. After all these years they're still sensitive about the revolting way the episode was handled. The man who found them acted as if a major crime had been committed. Suggested—although it was more like blackmail—that the senior reconsider his life and not corrupt the Air Force with his kind of preferences. It was right before graduation, the kid's parents were on their way to school, and the man wouldn't let up. The kid went over the brink. The current dean was still upset about it. Kept reassuring me that, even then, those attitudes were not representative of the college."

"And the boy's partner? Did they say anything?"

"Only that he was younger. He transferred to another school."

I smoothed down the programs, creasing and recreasing one of them. "Driving someone to suicide for something that's nobody's business, that hurt nobody. It's so ugly," I said.

"It probably threatened to become uglier. The junior, I assume, was the son of someone famous. The ex-governor of the state."

"But if nobody but that warped old man knew about it—"

"Obviously, people knew. A suicide can't be ignored. He left a note. Somebody found it. And the transferee was a badly shaken, lonely boy. He might have confided in a friend. A good friend." He stopped folding his fliers and looked at me. "A good friend who then becomes such a constant companion, everybody assumes she'll marry him."

"Still, even if Sissie knew, she's known all along. Why dredge up the story now?"

"We don't know that anyone did. But there might be other stories. And even if we all say a man's sexual preference is irrelevant, do you think it is, even today, to the electorate? Don't be an idealist—think of what just one story like that could do to a man's political ambitions."

We sat there quietly. I don't know what Mackenzie's mind was doing, but mine was pawing through the ragbag, pulling out remembered scraps and patches and trying to stitch them together into a pattern.

The purple lady saw only my inactive surface. "Finished?" she burbled, lifting the pile. "I can't *tell* you how grateful I am."

We both nodded humbly.

"But if you've a smidgen more time," she said, "we are still in such desperate need of help. Of course, we're grateful for all the donations, but people do not understand about bringing things in on time and tagging them, and—" She stopped, stammered a bit when she met Mackenzie's clear blue gaze. "Well," she said, "would you—could you carry some things up onto the platform?"

"In a minute, Ma'am," Mackenzie said, and once again the "Ma'am" soothed a savage breast. "But if you'll give us just a minute or so alone, we'd 'preciate it. You know how it is."

"Of course!" She backed off in a purple haze.

"I could hear you thinkin'," he said to me. "What'd you decide?"

"How does this sound? Hayden needs a wife for public relations purposes. He's getting too old to be unmarried and not suspect. Sissie, who understands the game, is willing to play, but she's still tangled in her marriage and off limits. Enter Liza, who has been pushed her whole life to be like the people her mother works for and worships, and who is impressionable. And then, before they marry, Sissie realizes she is no longer married and no longer rich. She nags at Hayden, but it doesn't work. So Sissie works on Liza and last Sunday they quarrel when Sissie plays her strongest hand. She tells Liza that Hayden's marrying her for political reasons, that she's a patsy, that Hayden doesn't like her or any woman. Tells her the college story or another one." I stopped, very tired.

"Go on, you're doing fine," Mackenzie said.

"But why isn't it fun when the puzzle comes together?"

Mackenzie just shrugged.

I forced myself on. All the little shreds had made a picture, but it was shabby and instantly stale. "Liza is playing her own game on the side with Eddie, but she doesn't like the idea of being used herself. Upset, she goes to Eddie after the show and tells him. And then —from then on it must have been all Eddie, C.K. And Eddie was scared by the murder and decided to come to me. But, by then, it was too late."

Mackenzie had made the mistake of looking toward the platform, and the purple woman was now gesticulating to us to come help. Mackenzie waved back at her in his dear, dumb way. "Why was Eddie scared?" he asked.

"The blackmail. The mother lode. The money thing. It would have been like Liza to make a scene and move away, go back to her original plan of moving to New York. I even think she told Sissie that, and Sissie thought the engagement was over. But Eddie must

have suggested using the information. Blackmailing
Hayden. So Liza went wandering around to think this
through, wound up at my house and..."

"Yes?"

"...called Hayden, and he killed her."

"Suddenly you don't like the idea? You sound disappointed, but isn't that what you've been pushing for?"

It wasn't anymore. I didn't want the killer to turn
out to be a victim as well. I didn't want it to be somebody running scared for years for no reason.

"You know," Mackenzie said, "Liza phoned Sissie that
morning, too. Maybe she returned the call, heard that
her tidy little scheme wasn't going to work that neatly.
If Liza destroyed Cole, Sissie would still be out one rich
husband. Maybe they quarreled."

"Do you think Hayden ever loved Liza?" The question, unanswered, depressed me more than anything
else. Had everything been based on a face-saving
nothingness? Wasn't passion involved anywhere?

"Who knows?" Mackenzie finally said. "Who is ever
going to know? Maybe he hoped he did. Or maybe it
was just politics."

"What happens now?"

"I don't know. Wouldn't it be nice to believe in the
old drawing room technique? Call them all into the
food booth after the auction and recite the known facts,
thereby forcing one of them to confess?"

"All? Isn't it either Hayden or Sissie?"

"All."

"But Gus has nothing to do with blackmail, or a
long-dead scandal, or—"

"And maybe that has nothing to do with what happened. I always pick up a lot of irrelevant and usually
ugly information. And speaking of picking things
up..."

He was looking at the platform. Other, more willing volunteers were dragging ill-assorted items up the steps and placing them on view. Next to the loaded make-shift platform stood Hayden Cole, looking himself like a worn antique that wouldn't fetch a decent price. As I watched, Sissie, still in costume, approached him. She took his palm and he smiled faintly. Perhaps she was teling his fortune, perhaps arranging it.

We walked slowly toward the next assignment.

"Fifteen minutes before the auction," the loud-speaker squawked. Other quitters straggled into our area and settled on the hard folding chairs. They car-ried balloons, stuffed toys, and sleeping babies.

The plump purple woman greeted us extravagantly. "Would you carry this up for me, dear?" she said, pointing to an oversized picture frame. "I've got tons more to arrange. Don't peek, though. It's an abso-lutely marvelous acrylic on velvet. The saddest-eyed boy and his puppy. My son painted it." She waltzed off with Mackenzie, explaining something intricate about the remainder of the folding chairs.

I stretched to get the ends of the package in my hands, and I staggered blindly toward the stage, man-aging to avoid too many collisions with people and chairs, finally making it up to the wooden platform. I found myself in a dog-eared treasure house. A lavabo lay on a drab piece of needlepoint; a set of tarnished candelabra poked out of the drawer of a chipped mahog-any drum table. On the podium, held down by the mike, a stack of certificates promised less tangible goodies. I flipped through them. Math tutoring, a casino weekend in Atlantic City, and, most intriguing, three free mar-riage-counseling sessions. I wondered what brave and shameless couple would bid on that one. I bet they'd say it was a gift for someone else.

I managed to control the urge to examine the sad-dest-eyed boy and his puppy, and I had started back down the steps when I heard voices floating up behind a curio cabinet.

Sissie's whisper was sporadically loud and intense. "It doesn't matter," she said. "Not to me."

Silence. I strained toward the cabinet.

"...don't know what you mean," Hayden said.

"We all make mistakes. What's past is past, Hayden."

He shushed her, and all I could hear were sibilant whispers, a great many of which sounded like the word "us."

I tiptoed down the steps.

"Miss Pepper. How do you do?" Hayden said from behind me. He looked at Sissie, then back at me and up to the platform. He didn't look serene.

Sissie held his arm possessively and she, too, glanced nervously from the platform to me.

"I'm bringing things up," I said gaily. "Really great things you have here." I hoped my wide-eyed admiration of the droppings of the gentry would convince the two of them that I heard and suspected nothing.

"Yes," Hayden agreed. "Interesting things up here. I'm keeping guard until we begin. Minding the shop, you might say." He released one brief, apologetic laugh.

Sissie let go her tentacles from Hayden's arm. "I'll call Mother Cole now, Hayden dear," she said. "I'm worried about her," she told me, as if I were suddenly a part of their group. She pulled off her black wig.

"Isn't your mother well?" I asked Hayden, trying to be polite.

"She's been very...shaken by Liza's..." His voice fogged. He cleared his throat.

I clucked sympathetically.

He looked grateful. "She wanted to come tonight. All her friends are here. But I discouraged it. The doctor's given her sedation. She would have liked talking to you. She looked for you yesterday, after the funeral."

I didn't dislike the man anymore. He had become human. He looked dangerously vulnerable, as if his former small share of spirit had oozed away. I watched him fold and unfold an auction program and had trouble imagining him bludgeoning anyone.

Sissie seemed annoyed by my presence. She stood, wig in hand, waiting for something. "Give Mrs. Cole my regards," I said, feeling like a fool.

Sissie nodded. "She'll appreciate that," she said, and she swished away.

"I'd better go help Mrs., ah, that woman in purple," I said because Hayden showed no sign of being able to end our awkward time together.

He nodded and continued smoothing the creases of his paper.

The program lady had me carry a porcelain vase that looked as if it had been through hard times, an enormous stuffed lion I was sure Karen would covet, and a basket of cheer containing wine, cheese, and crackers. I lusted for the third object, a quiet place, and Mackenzie, and I finally realized that I had no connection with Main Line Charities and had no need to continue working for them.

I went to resign, but the lady popped a stack of programs in my hand. "And since it was your marvelous idea," she chirped, "could you just give one to everybody?"

I stood in the chilly air like a zombie, handing out

programs. Finally, when he was sure he wasn't going to be asked to set up any more chairs, Mackenzie shambled over. I handed him the remaining programs.

"What's this?" he asked.

"Equal opportunity. I'll be right back. I absolutely must find a restroom and my sweater. It's in the car. Save me a place."

"Wait a minute." He looked at the programs as if they were a pestilence.

The bathrooms were a more popular attraction than the auction. The line, at least in front of the one cunningly labeled "Porta-Jane" was packed with women, young girls, and small boys who still needed their mother's assistance. I heard the auction begin in the distance. The missing gavel had obviously been found, because it was smacked down several times. "This... vase..." Hayden's electronically shored-up voice said. "Do I hear one dollar?"

When I came out, Hayden was still at it. "Do I hear ten? Fifteen? Seventeen?" I wondered if it was the same cracked piece of porcelain.

I shivered. I was near the parking lot behind the stores, and I walked toward Beth's station wagon. It was parked directly behind Denim Heaven, blocked in by a burgundy sedan. I wasn't pleased by the sight, since it meant we'd have to stay until the burgundy driver decided to leave. On the other hand, maybe Mackenzie would wrap things up or give up and whisk me off into the night.

I tried each handle of the car. Cautious Sam had locked them all. My red cardigan was a warm beacon on the back seat. I kept stupidly tugging on each door in turn and then, as I persisted, I had a feeling of déjà vu. The evening had dragged on, to be sure, but had I done this already?

I had, but not here. On Gus's car, in the rain, last Monday. My car had been blocking it.

I shivered from the cold, but I felt a warm surge of something near elation. Because if I was blocking Gus's car all day Monday, then he couldn't possibly have driven away during the day, and he couldn't possibly have walked on that bad leg to get to Liza. Now I had hard proof of what I'd known all along; he couldn't be a murderer.

I gave up on the sweater and walked quickly back in the direction of the supermarket, eager to tell Mackenzie. That, the memory of the blocked car, had been the thing I'd remembered and instantly forgotten Wednesday night when C.K.'s car blocked my street and the other driver honked. Nothing, however, would push it out of my mind this time.

I was near the market's solid brick side when a bulky figure came around its far corner. "Miss Pepper? Is that you?" Mrs. Cole made her way toward me. "I thought it was, but I wasn't sure. What a nice surprise!"

"I'm surprised, too," I said. "Your son said you weren't feeling well."

"Nonsense," she said emphatically, convincingly. "I am perfectly well."

And then she stepped off the narrow sidewalk that ran around the building, wobbled and toppled and collapsed onto the blacktop.

Sixteen

MY GOOD SAMARITAN INSTINCTS WERE HAM-
pered by the old woman's unyielding bulk. I fumbled
and faltered, she pulled and struggled, and we looked
like Laurel and Hardy in drag.

Finally, I had her standing up, braced against me.

"My ankle," she said in a surprised, small voice. The
lady was not used to leaning on anybody, and she kept
putting tentative pressure on the offending leg, wincing each time, then leaning on my shoulder once
again. Her right knee was scraped and slowly bleeding
onto her dress.

I didn't know what to do about her. I considered
dropping her onto the blacktop or propping her like a
piece of lumber against the supermarket wall. Both
ideas lacked a certain finesse.

"I look a mess," Mrs. Cole said.

Frankly, she hadn't been eligible for any best-dressed
lists before her tumble. Her flowery blue dress was the
pick of a litter of Main Line frumpies. Over it, she had
a slightly worn gray cashmere sweater and a patterned
lilac scarf that crisscrossed her ample bosom. But now,

her faded hair was rumpled, and the scrape on her knee oozed onto shredded stockings.

"I don't feel at all well," she added. "I should have stayed home."

"Do you think you could sit on the curb while I get help?" My shoulder throbbed. She had elected the already-damaged one as her makeshift crutch.

"What curb?" There was merit to her question. The curb was low and sporadically nonexistent as it dissolved into market-basket ramps. "I'm not a young woman, Miss Pepper."

"I'm sorry. I wasn't thinking clearly. But I should go get your son."

"Isn't he auctioneering now? I wouldn't want him to stop, make a fuss, and disrupt everything. He'd be so angry. I wasn't supposed to come. I wasn't supposed to drive, either." She winced again.

"Then I'll ask Sissie to come."

She shook her head. "Please. Sissie has Petey here and responsibilities, and she's just like family—she'd be angry because I sneaked out, didn't even have the driver bring me. Anyway, I would like to get out of these ripped stockings and get my ankle into some warm water. Could you possibly be very kind and drive me home? My house is nearby, in Ardmore. Five minutes away. You were there for the engagement party. You must remember."

Of course I did. Who would forget the hilltop palazzo? Its grounds were the size of territories that issue stamps.

"If you'd drop me off, my housekeeper would help me, and my driver would bring you back."

"But still, I should—"

"Ten minutes all told." She sounded very unlike herself, fragile and frightened. "Oh, please, Miss Pepper?"

There is just so much pressure from disabled old ladies that I can withstand while maintaining my self-respect. "Which way is your car?" I asked.

She gestured, grunting with each slow step we took, and we made our way across the supermarket lot and down a side street. Finally we reached her car, a discreetly weathered gray Mercedes. At least I was chauffeuring in style.

What an interesting line the Coles teetered on, wrangling for the popular vote, proclaiming democracy, while hanging on to every vestigial aristocratic right.

I helped Mrs. Cole onto the right front seat, and I settled in behind the wheel. The leather was soft and luxurious. She handed me the keys.

"That's it, you're doing fine," she said as I cautiously started the car and managed to pull away from the curb without denting the fender.

She fanned herself. "My! The exertion! I'm quite warm suddenly."

I was sweaty myself. I don't like to handle other people's valuables, let alone drive them. I concentrated on the car, on finding the turn signal and making a smooth right off Lancaster Avenue. I bade a silent farewell to the lights of the fair.

Mrs. Cole meanwhile fanned herself and removed the drab sweater and pale scarf, folding the latter into a tidy square.

"Do I turn at this light?" I asked.

She didn't seem to hear me, so I looked over, repeating myself. "Is it this next light or—" The words died as I viewed the newly revealed Mrs. Cole. Above the demure scoop of her blue frock, her bared neck bore the wattles and lines of age. But, more significantly, it also sported a small, filigreed locket.

She saw my stare, and she raised her hand protectively. "Next corner," she said in a flat voice. "Is something wrong?" She looked down, toward her hidden cleavage.

I concentrated on driving and on locking my bottom jaw back into place.

"Dear? You looked...startled."

"Oh, no," I said. "I was just admiring your locket. A student of mine, Stacy Felkin, has one just like it."

"I doubt that. Not like it at all." Her voice was at its most imperial, somewhat amused that anyone could presume her locket was one of a series. "It's quite impossible," she said. "This was Grandmother Lucy Bolt Hayden's, my dear. She gave it to my father, Benjamin Sedgewick Hayden."

What is "déjà vu" for sounds? I'd heard those words, that same voice saying them before. Or a voice giving a perfect imitation. Liza, in my classroom, mimicking this woman. And Liza, wearing that locket while she spoke. It had been given to her with that presentation speech.

"It's been in my family for generations," she said sweetly.

I could still hear and see Liza, hunched a bit, making her body bulky and putting a nasal edge on her voice. But long ago was long ago. Had she kept the locket? I tried to think about last Monday morning.

"You can drive a bit faster, dear. My ankle is more painful than I realized at first."

"I'm a little nervous."

"Why?"

"The, ah—car. I've never driven a Mercedes before. Kind of intimidating." I tugged out every memory of Monday morning. I remembered Liza's gestures as she smoked and fidgeted with her hair, with her T-

shirt, and with something at her neck. A glinting, gold
thing. The locket. She always wore it. That's why
Stacy imitated it.

She was wearing it Monday morning.

But was she wearing it when I found her? I forced
myself back over every second of that nightmare home-
coming. I had buried the memory as far away as I
could, but I forced myself to look at it, at her again. I
had put my head on her chest, listening for a heartbeat. Was there a locket nearby? Could I feel its pressure on my temple? Could I see it at all?

"Turn right here, dear. The light's green."

I crept along.

Maybe the police had returned the locket to the family. Maybe I shouldn't be leaping to conclusions.

Mrs. Cole was tidying up, shuffling around in her
brown purse, putting away the folded scarf.

The ring had been on Liza's hand. I remembered the
police mentioned it, and I saw it, too. But the ring was
new and hadn't mattered to the Coles. Liza had said so.

Mrs. Cole held her hand up to her neck protectively
again. "My grandmother, Lucy Bolt Hayden, was a fine
woman," she murmured, her voice placid and self-satisfied. "And her father was a great man." She sounded
almost like someone telling herself a beloved fairy tale.

I tried to sort out the questions bombarding my
brain. I couldn't think coherently with Mrs. Cole doing
her genealogical monologue and my consciousness di-
vided into the figuring-out part and the driving part, so
I pulled over to the side of the road. Nobody passed
us. Not one single moving vehicle troubled the Coles'
neighborhood with noise and exhaust fumes.

"Don't stop the car," Mrs. Cole said. "My ankle—"

"I'm dizzy for some reason." Mackenzie! Mackenzie,
we talked through the entire crime, except we didn't

realize that the necklace was a clue. Was it on the body when I found it?

Mrs. Cole stared at me intently.

I saw myself again, and again, bending over Liza, shaking her. I saw her head wobble.

There hadn't been anything on that slender neck.

"Do you feel better now?" Mrs. Cole asked.

I nodded.

Would Hayden have removed the locket and returned it to his mother?

No. Nobody attached that degree of significance to it except the woman beside me. She had taken it herself. She had watched Liza die, waited for her to die, and then taken the locket.

I shuddered.

"Are you well?" Mrs. Cole asked.

"Chilly," I said, fearing that my teeth were going to chatter. I thought of Mrs. Cole staring impassively at Liza and tried not to think of Mrs. Cole, now staring at me with mild and distant interest.

"Then please start driving again," Mrs. Cole said. "I'll put the heater on if you're cold."

I put the car into gear once more.

She didn't know that I knew anything about the locket. I was safe. Innocent. I repeated the idea to myself several times. We passed the train station and crossed under the tracks of the Main Line of the railroad. We were now on the right side of the tracks. Literally. The Cole house was very near here, looming somewhere above our tree-lined, meandering road.

I glanced down at Mrs. Cole's ankle. It looked just as it had before, swaddled in its wrinkled stocking. Shouldn't it be swelling? Had she hurt it at all?

She swiveled toward me, using the "wounded" foot as a pivot, and I had my answer.

Why had she gotten me into her car? Why did she want me in her house? I didn't think we had a similar conception of what could provide an evening's amusement.

"How provident to find you on the parking lot," Mrs. Cole murmured. "Turn right at the end of this road. We're around that bend and off to the left."

She took that locket off Liza's neck, my brain said with finality. It printed it in caps. In neon.

SHE MURDERED LIZA.

I was near the corner. She murdered Liza. She murdered Eddie. Even an old lady can push. Even an old lady can pour boiling water. Even an old lady can tape newspaper headlines on a piece of paper and shove it through a mail slot. She knew I was at the carnival. Sissie phoned her. I sent regards. The only surprise was that I was right there for her on the lonely parking lot.

I turned left.

She is going to murder me.

I sped by the long entryway to the Coles' estate.

"You've missed it! You missed the turn after I clearly—"

"I'm sorry! I'll get us right back."

But not back here. Back to the fair. I needed Mackenzie, who was undoubtedly sitting calmly at the auction, covering his Big Three suspects. Dear God, but we'd been stupid. Even the detective with his revealed truths. We'd figured out the probable why of the murders, but goofed by a mile on the who.

So now I was driving a two-time murderer around, and I believed the superstition that bad things go in threes. But still, the idea was ludicrous, because what did she want of me? She could, after all, have mugged me on the parking lot, if that was her ambition.

"What are you doing?" Mrs. Cole snapped. "There's no need to creep along this way."

"I have night blindness."

"You saw well enough when you raced past my house."

"Mrs. Cole, I'm not feeling well. I'm driving back to the fair. Hayden can take you home." My teeth chattered, giving my act some credibility.

"You'll do no such thing. Drive me back to my road and take me home."

I shook my head, my teeth clattering away.

"Well," she said with something like a genteel snort, "we're not so sweet anymore, are we? You're behaving very oddly, Miss Pepper. Why don't you just say what's on your mind? And meanwhile, turn this car around and do as I say."

"Nothing's on my mind." I leaned over the steering wheel, peering into the dark, winding road.

"Oh, yes it is. You lie just the way she did. No wonder you were such good friends. Confidantes. You're as much a liar as she was. Everything she said was a filthy lie, and she didn't care that it would ruin my son, my plans, my name."

I half expected her to mention her country and her universe as being at risk. But more upsetting than her overuse of personal pronouns was that she was admitting much too much to me. I did not want to hear any of it—at least not in these close quarters.

"Mrs. Cole," I said in a soothing voice, "you're upset. You've hurt yourself, and you're feeling poorly. I don't know what lies you're talking about, but if they're important, perhaps you should tell the police, not me."

I continued creeping along, waiting for a turn that would bring me back toward Lancaster Avenue.

"The police? What have I to do with the police?"

I saw a turn ahead and I moved more quickly, then swung the steering wheel to the right.

"What are you doing?" Her voice had become shrill, a bit less cultivated. "This is the wrong way—"

But she was too late. The car sped ahead, down an incline and into the rain-swollen stream. This was not the time to discuss the peculiarities of the Main Line street system that includes a road that fords a stream. I crashed into the water and back up again onto dry land.

"Turn around right now. You get us back right now," she ordered. "Right here, right now!" She waved her hand at the window.

I kept on going. Her one clear goal was to have me at her house, and I wasn't going.

"I won't—" she began.

"The brakes are wet. I can't slow down. I can't turn." In the distance, behind acres of trees and green gardens, I thought I could make out the bright lights of my destination.

"You'll take me home!" she repeated, rustling through her purse again. Her voice was no longer shrill or ruffled. It was smug and secure. As well it might be, considering what possession she now chose to show me.

A gun in the hand is worth a lot of self-confidence.

"Mrs. Cole! What are you doing?"

She sighed. "I didn't want it this way. But I must finish it tonight."

"By—by shooting me?"

"Not unless you make it necessary."

"It isn't! It's not at all necessary. It won't accomplish a thing."

She shook her head. "Of course it would. It would stop the chain. End this business. Avoid shame."

She was insane. But so was I, because I kept trying to reason with a madwoman. "Mrs. Cole, the police—"

"They know nothing. Not with Liza, not with that—that henchman of hers." She pushed the gun into my rib cage. "Now drive me home," she said calmly. "I don't want to shoot you, but I will if you don't cooperate."

I nodded emphatically. Far be it from me to coerce someone into destroying my vital organs. "The next possible turn," I whispered. "What henchman?" I added. "What do you mean?" Perhaps I could get her so involved in her own story that she would momentarily forget about the gun in my side. I made my face wide open and expectant, ready to be informed.

She chuckled nastily. "I've never appreciated your innocent act, but this time it's silly. You know who it was. You led me to him, Miss Pepper."

I was momentarily diverted, dazzled by her politeness. She would call me by my full name even while planning to kill me. Breeding certainly does tell.

"Him? Who?" My voice, when it returned, squeaked, but she didn't mind.

"Eddie, of course. When Liza, when she was, well, upset, she tried to threaten me, said Eddie knew everything and he'd get me. I didn't know who or what she meant. But I knew you would know. You were her closest friend. She stayed with you so often, confided in you. So I wasn't surprised when I heard you say 'Eddie' at the viewing, and when I heard him say something about Liza. Sissie told me the rest of his name. I thought he might really know something, have something. But there was nothing there. Just his insinuations. They were two of a kind. Trash. Dirt. Nothings."

She leaned back, looking at the roof of the car but keeping the gun at my side. I tried to comfort myself

with reminders that guns were not her weapon of
choice, and since there was no fireplace or boiling kettle around, I was probably safe.

"The problem was," she said, "somebody might have
believed them all the same. She was a convincing little
actress. Threatening me with a press conference! De-
manding money! She should have been grateful for
what Hayden and I were doing for her. Instead, she
was ready to ruin him and everything we stand for.
She said we had used her, as if she were something
valuable. But of course you know all that. It was even
your house she chose for her disgusting act."

She listed her grievances with gusto, giving me time.

"I didn't know she was going to call you," I said,
playing her game.

"She didn't. She called Hayden, but he wasn't home. I
returned the call, invited her to lunch. I was polite and
gracious. And she said she should have called me in the
first place because I would do just fine. She wanted to
talk, she said. Talk! Threaten! Lie!"

I could see Mrs. Cole arriving at my house, dressed
in a spring luncheon ensemble, a flowered hat on her
head and white gloves. A gentlewoman in gloves
wouldn't leave prints.

"Get me home."

For her own obscure reasons, Mrs. Cole didn't want
to kill me while we were driving. If need be, I would
therefore drive throughout eternity. "That's a one-way
street," I said, passing a possible turnoff.

"Oh." Mrs. Cole's voice was small and obedient. She
only broke the big laws.

"Mrs. Cole," I said calmly, "how can you possibly
benefit by doing...this?" I didn't yet know what "this"
might be, so I left it vague, unwilling to plant ideas in
her mind, although the gun at my side did indicate a

certain seriousness of purpose. "You aren't protecting your son or his name if you—"

"Of course I'm protecting my son. He doesn't deserve it, the fool. I've spent my life saving him, pushing and prodding and having to take care of his every move. He hasn't got his father's courage, his family's ambition. He's...angry with me now. Suspicious."

"Then if you—if I—if something happens, he'll tell the police."

"No," she said firmly. "I know him. He won't do a thing."

We were seconds away from Lancaster Avenue and relative safety, or at least noise and light. I felt as if years had passed since I'd gotten into this car, but I realized it had been only a matter of minutes. Maybe Mackenzie wasn't even suspicious. Maybe he thought a woman could primp for hours in a Porta-Jane.

But I needed only a little bit more time. "Mrs. Cole, even if he won't do anything, the police will know who... did it to me." My voice trailed off. It is difficult to discuss one's own untimely death in a detached, clinical manner.

"They will not know a thing."

"But this is your car. That is your gun. You won't get away with it."

"I have no intention of getting away with anything. Just of getting on with it. We are both going to die and end this entire business once and for all. You have to die. You know too much. But I will not go to prison, Miss Pepper. Coles do not go to prison."

As interesting sociologically as that last idea was, I had another, more pressing line of questions.

"How?" I whispered. "How are we...going to...?"

"There is a dangerous, unfortunate embankment on the approach to my house. We're going over it. You'll already be dead, you see. I will then set the car in position, use the gasoline I have ready in the trunk and release the brake. An accident, that's all. Ascribable to my sedation, perhaps."

"They'll wonder why I was there," I began.

"Let them wonder!"

That about ended that avenue of thought. I tried a new tack, a few civilized words against the project. I'd appeal to her patrician standards. "Mrs. Cole, it's a foolish, meaningless, vile thing to do!"

"Foolish? Vile? How dare you speak to me that way?"

"How can you dare try to kill me! You can't go around pushing people any which way. You're no better than anyone else. You have no more rights than I do." I kept driving and spouting elements of democracy, knowing I sounded like a fool, but a gun in one's side can wreak havoc with one's rhetoric.

"You—you're just like her," she said, her skin mottling. The gun wavered, lost pressure. She pulled in her breath in a broken, quivering gasp and steadied herself. The gun went back into position, more deeply, pressing hard and painfully against my rib cage.

The light was green ahead. I floored the accelerator, turned right, and looked with adoration at the carnival lights winking and blinking up ahead.

"Get off this street!" she screamed. "Do you hear me? You take me home this instant!"

But no matter what I'd ever said, I wanted to spend Saturday night at the fair, and I was going to. I took a deep breath in preparation for the next two blocks. "Thanks for the invitation," I said calmly, "but I'd feel out of place at your house, so I'm not coming over tonight."

"That's very unwise, Miss Pepper. But it doesn't matter. I see that now. I can be flexible. You'll die now instead of later. I have nothing to lose either way."

The gun left my ribs, and I turned. Mrs. Cole's eyes were fierce, fanatical. She bit her lip to steady herself as she raised the barrel to my head.

"Don't do it," I said.

"Don't tell me what to do." She squinted and took a deep breath. She was probably yearning for something to bash me with. Guns weren't her things.

We were chugging away in deep fast traffic. I was afraid to slam on the brakes and leap out because I couldn't judge the impact of the gun pointing at me, but it seemed a tossup between being shot in the side or the back, depending on how quickly I moved. I had long since known that logic had no place in the woman's thinking.

"*Nobody* tells me what to do," she said. Her breath was somewhat labored.

She was right. Nobody did. Not ever. I suddenly saw Liza and Eddie, both paralyzed by bedrock politeness, stunned like animals in headlights while the little old lady advanced, aristocratic, regal, unshakable, and elderly. A deadly combination.

I had no time and only one possible weapon.

"Screw you, bitch!" I screamed at the top of my lungs. "Who the hell are you? You're nothing, and you're nobody! You're a murderer! You're *trash!*"

Her nostrils flared, her mouth opened speechlessly. Nobody had ever spoken to her that way. Nobody had spoken to her parents or grandparents that way. I had just upended the rule of generations. She gaped in wonder.

I seized the moment. I smacked down at the gun and it fell, heavily, across my right foot.

I reached for it, but so did she. I gave her first dibs.

I lifted my foot and stomped as hard as I could, down onto her hand as it stretched across the accelerator.

We took off, beginning the first Lancaster Avenue Grand Prix.

"You can't!" she screamed, breathing heavily, clawing at my leg with her free hand, twisting to pull herself free of my foot.

"I can! I am!" I shouted as we zoomed through the intersection. "I'm not dying for your honor or anything else!" Where was a cop when I needed one? I wanted to be pulled over, arrested, lectured, put on trial. Rescued. But instead, cars honked and people shouted, and I headed for the carnival's lights. "Please, God," I said as shops and sidewalks blurred by, "everybody be at the auction, because—" I turned the wheel to the right, sharply.

She screamed, bringing her left arm up to my face, banging my head against the window. Her fingers clawed at my eyes. She was incredibly strong and agile.

The steering wheel in my left hand convulsed, but I couldn't think about it as I pried her fingers. There was a part of me still fixated on the fact that she was an old woman—not a fierce male attacker, against whom I could be ruthless.

And then I mentally said what the hell and bit down on her hand until she yelped and yowled and pulled it away. For a flash, before the fist was back, hitting and pounding my temple, I saw Beth's food stand zoom directly toward the windshield. I pulled at the wheel, but not enough. We amputated its right side. Glass and food flew into the air, over the car.

There was no time for regrets. We were heading toward—we were in and through—a game booth. Stuffed tigers and elephants banged onto the hood and ricocheted onto the ground. I didn't know where to turn. We neared the edge of the carnival, but I wasn't going to leave it. I might die there, but I wouldn't leave it. I turned the wheel again, never releasing pressure on Mrs. Cole's hand and the accelerator.

"Let me go!" she screamed. She started to cry, and she sounded like an angry child having a tantrum. "Let me go! Let me go! Let me go!"

The silent merry-go-round was directly ahead. I pulled violently on the wheel to get the car onto the walkway.

But nobody had designed the carnival for a runaway Mercedes. I heard a heartrending scream of metal against wood, and the car ground to a halt. The passenger side was now part of the decoration of the calliope, and a wide-eyed silver horse looked in through the smashed side window.

It was time to leave.

I threw open my car door and ran toward the supermarket, the auction, people, screaming for help. How could they not have heard the crash? How could the auction be so compelling that they'd stay with it through this?

My screams were drowned out by the sounds of more metal being loosened, more glass and wood crushing as the car started up again.

I ran faster.

Then suddenly, I was bathed in light. I turned and saw headlights, or one headlight, coming toward me. The Cole car was designed to last as long as the name. Nothing could stop it or its driver. Not a side door hanging loose. Not broken glass or garlands of doll innards and food. It was still running and it was aimed directly at me.

I ran toward the shops, the pavement at the back of the fair, then sideways, toward the auction.

She would get me, I suddenly knew. Whatever confidence and bravado I'd clung to disappeared, washed out in the headlight. She would crush me against the shops, killing us both, as she'd always intended.

And then the militia arrived.

I heard it before I saw it. Footsteps, screams, shouts. Hundreds of feet, chairs toppling far away and above it, over the microphone, Hayden's voice shouting desperately, "Calm down everyone. Let the security people find out what—calm down, please."

"Terrorists!" a woman shouted. "Bombs!" another voice said.

People who had run toward the rubble shrieked. I didn't stop to console them or to apologize. I headed straight into the mass of the crowd and kept running.

He was maybe the tenth person I passed. "Amanda!" he shouted. "Amanda!" He grabbed my shoulders and held on. It was hard for me to stop my feet. "Whaaa...whasit...ahbe..." His words blurred into one stunned drawl.

"It's her. It was her all along. She's going to—get these people back or she'll kill us all! She doesn't care!"

"Who? What?"

I waved my hand behind me, then turned.

The car was gone.

A security guard appeared from behind Denim Heaven. He coughed apologetically. "I—there seemed nothing I could do when I saw what was..." He stopped and waited for us to make him feel better.

Mackenzie glared at the man, looked at me, looked at the dark sky. Then he spoke. "Yay-uss. Well, now you can just go call the local police." The man slinked off.

A second guard, pale and shaken, waved his gun in the air from his hiding place nearby. "Gone!" he shouted. "Drove right through!" He pointed to the ruins of a booth. The ground was wet and covered with tiny goldfish. They should have let us catch them earlier.

"She killed them, too," I said. "Killed them all. Mrs. Cole. She's the guilty one. Except they were all ambitious, and who's to say? That's a good question. If you were to judge, then who? Liza? Macbeth? Eddie? Fate?"

"Are you all right?" He held me close. "It's over," he whispered. "You're safe. You solved it. You're the heroine of the day."

"All the same," I said, "I need a minute or two to collapse. Cry. Disintegrate." Which I did, more or less, and he held me, making low, soft sounds of Southern comfort until I was calm again.

"Come with me," he said then. "I have to take care of some things, but I don't want to leave you."

"You don't have to. You don't have to leave me. You don't have to stop her. She'll take care of it herself."

"How can you be sure?"

"She told me. She won't face the shame. She has a gun. Dear God, this is so ugly. Every piece of it, even now, her last face-saving."

The local police arrived before the guard's call summoned them. The echoes of the premature dismantling of the Main Line Charities Carnival had reached them. They left in pursuit of the decrepit gray Mercedes.

I became aware of two silent people nearby. Sissie, in her scarlet dress but without her wig, looked stunned. "Mother Cole?" she repeated several times to herself. She looked at Hayden. "I thought that..." Then she decided to let it go, and she stood, shaking her head.

Hayden said nothing. Perhaps his mother had been right. Perhaps he never would say anything, but his ashen face spoke volumes. I turned away from both of them.

"Can you talk about it now?" C.K. asked, and I nodded. I explained to him, then again to Beth and Sam, and then to a local policeman, what had just happened. By the third retelling, I got the thing down to a size where I could handle it. There were even parts I could laugh at.

"So now you have a story for your twilight years," Mackenzie said as we got into his car later. "I can just see you with your great-grandchildren. 'Hey, Granny,' they'll say, 'tell us again how you stopped the crazy lady from shooting you.'"

"And I'll say, 'Kiddies, sometimes it pays to have no class.'"

"They never taught us about disarming somebody by bein' uppity," Mackenzie said.

"There are lots of things you didn't learn at the police academy, Coriolanus. How lucky for you, then, to be in the company of one of the world's finest teachers. And I do private tutoring, at home. I'm alive, and you're alive, and there's still enough weekend left in which to celebrate the fact of life."